MOUNTAIN

Copyright © 2017 Ursula Pflug

Except for the use of short passages for review purposes, no part of this book may be reproduced, in part or in whole, or transmitted in any form or by any means, electronically or mechanically, including photocopying, recording, or any information or storage retrieval system, without prior permission in writing from the publisher or a licence from the Canadian Copyright Collective Agency (Access Copyright).

 Canada Council Conseil des Arts
for the Arts du Canada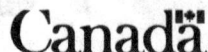

We gratefully acknowledge the support of the Canada Council for the Arts and the Ontario Arts Council for our publishing program. We also acknowledge the financial support of the Government of Canada through the Canada Book Fund.

Cover design: Val Fullard

Mountain is a work of fiction. All the characters and situations portrayed in this book are fictitious and any resemblance to persons living or dead — with the exception of historical personages — is purely coincidental.

Library and Archives Canada Cataloguing in Publication

Pflug, Ursula, 1958-, author
    Mountain / a novel by Ursula Pflug.

(Inanna young feminist series)
Issued in print and electronic formats.
ISBN 978-1-77133-349-8 (softcover).-- ISBN 978-1-77133-350-4 (epub).
-- ISBN 978-1-77133-351-1 (Kindle).-- ISBN 978-1-77133-352-8 (pdf)

    I. Title. II. Series: Inanna young feminist series

PS8581.F58M69 2017   jC813'.6   C2017-900322-4
                                                                                        C2017-900323-2

Printed and bound in Canada

Inanna Publications and Education Inc.
210 Founders College, York University
4700 Keele Street, Toronto, Ontario, Canada M3J 1P3
Telephone: (416) 736-5356 Fax: (416) 736-5765
Email: inanna.publications@inanna.ca   Website: www.inanna.ca

MOUNTAIN

URSULA PFLUG

Young Feminist Series

ALSO BY URSULA PFLUG

NOVELS
Motion Sickness
The Alphabet Stones
Green Music

SHORT FICTION
Harvesting the Moon
After the Fires

To my aunt Michaela, in gratitude

ou stacked them they'd get knocked over and would be where. "You think this is party time," my mother said, ng to face me. "Like all the other places we've been. But ot. This gathering is different."

ce I didn't much enjoy the other so-called gatherings had been to, I wasn't impressed. "Different from getting ?" I asked.

My mother was lighting her blue clay pipe, a present from rk. "There's gatherings every year on this mountain in the ring. They say it's a holy place, brings necessary changes," aureen persisted.

"They?" I asked.

"The people who come," Laureen said. "The Tribe."

We waited while the guy ran back for another plank. It was bright outside, but dark in the cab, so I couldn't make out Laureen's face as she offered me the pipe. "It will heal your bones," she said.

"My bones are the least of my problems," I said. "And you know I can't take your healing talk seriously after what happened."

"What happened?" Laureen asked.

"With Peter," I said.

Laureen stared at me for a long time. Then she abruptly changed the subject, a thing she'd done often, to my eternal consternation. "That's Skinny," she said, catching me watching the guy who was coming toward us again. "He's Tribe, too."

"Too?" I asked.

"As is your mother. Meaning me," Laureen said.

"My," I said. "Another accomplishment. You have so many. Whatever Tribe is."

My eyes were drawn back to the guy. "Shut up, Nan," he was saying to the cursing woman. "It's Laureen. Look, Laureen's here."

1

VERY EARLY MORNING, the night's rain was dripping from everything standing, its rhythm a backdrop to my first fatigue-warped vision of camp. My eyes were grainy from lack of sleep and secretly I cursed Laureen, wished I'd gone east to Lark after all, back when the truck first broke down in B.C. My mother could've come down here alone.

Winter's ice was coming unstuck under the April sun, washing down the mountain through the camp. I'd been to the mountains before, knew even at noon it would still be cold under the Ponderosas, among the crates of vegetables sunk for refrigeration into white hips of remaining snow. Next to the kitchen tent, a creek ran under the picnic tables; except it wasn't really a creek, just runoff in a gravelly gully. Pieces of the mountain, ground down by ice.

A youngish guy in a white T-shirt sat on a picnic table paring apples. Bushels of apples, gone soft and bruised over the winter, good only for cooking with now. "Laureen!" he called, seeing us, waving his skinny arms in greeting.

My mother swore, spun her wheels. He grabbed a board from a pile and came running over with it. I stared, wondering how he wasn't cold; even with my jean jacket on I was still shivering. A woman started cursing for the missing plank. I could see how without shelves to sit on, the cardboard boxes of beans would soak through in a minute, and then no matter

The woman stopped what she was doing to stare at us. "Fuck Laureen," she said, full of animosity, turning back to her work.

My mother smiled at Skinny, her first smile since Vancouver, since the truck broke down the second time. I was beginning to think she was sour always: sour I couldn't drive or change tires or push the truck very well when it got stuck. Sour I burnt the food and didn't have enough money to take my bad moods back east to Lark on my own.

Last night when we pulled over, moonlight through windy pines strobed the wall of mountain blasted away to build a midnight coast road; so beautiful I was briefly happy. Still snow where in only another month everything would be brown and dry, or was that farther south in California?

There were other journeys west for my mother and me. Sometimes now the years and trips blur together and it's only people's faces that remain etched into the softened blacktop of events. Everything runs together: which route we took; which country we were in, ours or theirs; the brown hills outside the car windows a marker of a border crossed, the little route numbers marking the roads taken, the years passed and gone.

There I was, being eloquent in my own head. I figured it must be my mother's pot, filling up the cab and my brain.

"You didn't answer me," I said.

"About what?" Laureen asked.

"You know about what."

Laureen looked out the window so I couldn't read her face. "This country is so beautiful to me because I see it so rarely. It's always a respite, a reprieve from the east." Laureen is wordy when stoned like me, only she's not so self-conscious that she keeps it to herself, like I do. "They run a drug free operation here," she rambled on evasively, "have to, to get permits. Skinny, you old son of a bitch," she said, turning her attention to the guy. Leaning out of the window she laughed while he stuck a second board under our wheels. Success! She came free and pulled us up onto dry land, turned the motor off, jumped out and threw her arms around Skinny. He threw his, too.

"Laureen, where you been all year?" he asked. "Remember in Vic with Dwayne and Sarah and Estevan? Have you seen them? How are they? Do they write? Where did you come from, today? Did you drive far?"

"I remember," my mom said, thumping his back. "And Felicity and Johann and Jean-Marc. You look great, Skinny, just great." I got out too, stood respectfully back, staring at the line of trees. The smell of pot hanging everywhere in spite of the regulations; several hundred people camped in a mud puddle with bad food and no medical. By week's end we'd all have scabies and staph infections running down our legs and die. I pretended not to watch Skinny and Laureen hug and kiss. Old lovers, for sure. Laureen would ignore me now, and I'd have to navigate this maze alone.

But Skinny had stepped back from Laureen to look at me, and then my mother walked away to go talk to someone else. It happens every time.

2

H E WASN'T SO TALL exactly as extremely thin and had shaved his head recently; his hair was only just starting to grow in. His skin was so pale I thought he must be a redhead; his fuzz so short it was hard to tell what colour it was. A sun-freckled nose turned up at the end like a kid's, but his eyes were the most surprising. Such a dark brown they appeared all pupils, but seemed to show emotion all the same. One emotion, I should say: mirth.

"You're Laureen's daughter. I know she must've told me, but I forget your name, how old you are; all that stuff. You been out West before?"

Why did his eyes laugh, I found myself wondering.

I answered the last question first. "Laureen comes more than I do. She worked with this famous designer Estevan again, all last year up in Vic. Oh, but I guess you know that part, you were there too. I remember that now. I live with my dad in Toronto, go to high school. This year I left early, so I could travel with mom. I'm sixteen," I added, which was the truth, and "my name's Camden," which was not. I never go by Amethyst. Even Crystal would've been better; I could've changed the spelling to its European counterpart, Krystle. Very traditional, nothing new-agey about it. "It's the name of the part of London I was born in," I lied again, idiotically.

Skinny nodded. "Nice name," he said, still staring. I figured the stare meant he knew me for a liar; Camden Town is actually the name of a song my father wrote me on the back of a postcard from England, on tour a few years ago. It was a minor hit and I remember my friends envied me for that but I just wished he'd come home. I'd stay with Laureen when he was away and sometimes we'd fight. Because of all those things, Camden Town marked my life. Some tattoos are names, so are some events. I didn't feel so bad about lying once I'd figured that out.

"It's all coming back to me now," Skinny said. "Your dad is Lark O'Connor. What's it like having a rock star for a dad?"

"He's pretty small time really," I said, trying to weigh whether Skinny was impressed or not. "But he's the purveyor of almost everything decent in my life, namely pizza, rock T-shirts, nice jeans, and concert and airline tickets."

I thought I'd managed to sound a tad ironic but all the same Skinny just muttered, "Things of great value."

I winced again but went on bravely, "I'd much rather be back east with him than out here, but Laureen insisted I go with her this time, and besides, Lark's recording and wouldn't have time for me anyway."

"And what do you make of your mother?" Skinny asked me.

"She smokes too much pot," I said.

Skinny laughed. "If that's the worst thing you can say about your mother, I suppose you two are still doing all right."

I looked around for the mother in question, hoping she'd come rescue me from this awkward conversation, but she was nowhere in sight; there was just mountain everywhere I looked. There were no flat places to stand; one foot was always higher than the other. Alpine meadow full of snow, mostly tramped into mud now. Tents spotted among the pines, people hunkered under their flies, trying to start fires with wet kindling, or hanging wet sleeping bags on lines strung between trees, pissed off. There was mist everywhere, rising from the ground. Still farther up, more people, sitting up on logs to keep out of the mud. Up there the snow banks weren't just in the woods but also on slopes that didn't face the sun. Go up two hundred metres, and you're in a different microclimate.

"It's pretty, isn't it?" he asked.

"Sure," I said, "Pretty snow waiting to be melted, make more mud."

My sarcasm usually throws people, but it had no effect on this guy, least not on his laughing eyes. I wondered if anything did.

"Your mother didn't even park the goddamn truck properly," he said. "If she comes back, get the keys and put it over there. That's the parking lot, eh?" Love that *eh*. It was his Victoria time showing, or maybe he was actually Canadian, like me.

"Yeah, sure," I said. "If I could drive."

Skinny stared at me as though it was astounding, that I didn't drive. "You do anything useful?" he asked. "Or just your nails?"

Mine were ice blue. Revlon double coat, a present from Lark. I'd done them yesterday, while Laureen changed tires again. They were only a little chipped. I know what that sounds like, but you don't know Laureen.

Towards the end she was even begrudging me a place to sleep. I remember one night last week, I think we were in Oregon, Oregon or Washington. She'd pulled the truck onto a side road, too fried to drive any longer. Sometimes we did that, slept on side roads. It was cheaper than camping passes even. "Without you I'd have the whole cab to myself for a bed," she'd said, tilting her seat back as far as it would go before she grabbed a quilt and closed her eyes.

"I'll sleep in the back," I'd offered, knowing the box leaked and I'd be wet. Laureen had only glared at me.

Skinny seemed to have forgotten he'd just insulted me. He turned to look at the so-called parking lot, at the edge of still more dripping Ponderosa pines. "*Voyez le stationnement! Et là-bas, beaucoup de granolas,*" he said, pointing and laughing.

His accent was worse than mine, but I had to ask. "You speak French?"

"Not really," Skinny said. "I went to one of Elder Commanda's gatherings in Quebec with Estevan years ago. Picked up a little."

There were a lot of old boards down in the parking area so the vehicles wouldn't go waist deep in muck, but of course the mud was just squelching up between the planks. The sight of the parking lot made me miss Lark's newish Subaru with something close to pain. Falling apart cars and trucks; big ugly biker-looking guys arguing tranny repair procedures, looking under hoods, lying on their backs underneath their vehicles, getting mud in their long filthy hair. They all made Skinny look positively angelic. *Beaucoup de granolas,* I only wished.

Suddenly Laureen was back. "How many people you got?" she demanded of Skinny. "Looks to me like three, four hundred. Not much for this late date, not much for a Tribe thing." She looked at her watch. "You guys are slipping, Security. You don't even have Kitchen going, yet."

"Maybe not but you've got a watch on," Skinny said.

My mother stared at him.

"Screws up your electromagnetic field," he said. "As any healer of any modality can tell you. You'll be nicer with it off, I'll bet."

Laureen looked horrified and took her watch off, tucking it into a pocket of her fraying down vest. "I've been driving too long," she apologized. "And in the city too long before that. So anyway," she said, switching to shop talk, "where's the hardware?"

You either love my mother or hate her and what with all

the hugs and kisses Skinny definitely seemed to be part of the first club. "You know so much, Laureen," he kidded. "You go over there and talk to Daniel."

He pointed to a huddle by the line of conifers. Daniel, it seemed, was yet another tall, ugly, bearded man speaking in hushed tones to an assembled group of minions.

"Daniel who?" Laureen said. "I've never heard of him."

"Me either. Someone Estevan recommended. He's from the south, Mississippi or Arkansas or someplace."

"That's a good sign," Laureen said. "They've been broker down there for longer, had to learn more the hard way."

"Indeed," Skinny said. "So, apparently he knows his shit. Especially good at bicycle-powered sound stages."

Laureen snorted. "Sound stages? Who the fuck cares? What does he think this place even is, a frickin' rock show? Hey, Daniel," she yelled.

Daniel looked, wasn't impressed, and turned back to his little group.

My mother strode across the field; her too big black rubber boots going *squish squish squish*. She got to the circle. She must have been yelling, because I could hear her clear as day from where I was standing. "Hey, Daniel. You listen when I talk to you. Don't you know who the fuck I am? I'm Laureen, man. Does that name mean anything to you?"

There was a touch of humour in her words, just enough. All the same, at first I was afraid he was going to hit her, or ignore her entirely. Thing is, Laureen doesn't look scary, but she doesn't look like someone you can ignore either. My tiny middle-aged mother stood there, dressed as always in a faded floral dress, a stained down vest, barn boots. Her long brown ringlets looked like their weeks on the road, not that Daniel's hair was any cleaner. But oddly her routine seemed to work and I wondered whether she'd tried it before on guys like that.

He clapped her on the back, laughing, introduced her to his people in low venerable tones.

Skinny watched me watching. "Laureen's really shy and she tries to fight it," he said. "Sometimes her trying to fight it comes out a little weird."

That was strange, him saying something insightful about Laureen. It was like he knew my mom better than I did. "So explain why the biker didn't hit her," I said.

Skinny laughed. "Her legend precedes her. Your mom can be a royal pain, but she's still the best."

3

TEN YEARS AGO I moved in with Lark and his model of the year, while my mother left for British Columbia to study with Estevan White. Estevan runs a renewable energy co-op, as well as a school in DIY design and implementation. In spite of being a woman, my mom's a hardcore hardware geek. She was his best student ever, or so she says he says. It must have been at least partly true, because now she travels around, getting paid just enough, to design and install the portable power stations and water purifiers and satellite linkups and things at these gatherings.

Skinny excused himself and went back to the kitchen tent, moved boxes around. Nobody noticed me. After my shoes were wet through, I went and sat down on a picnic bench under the fly. It was one of those big open sided things, utilitarian beige canvas, like the army or boy scouts have. Skinny and a hippie-looking woman kept moving boxes from one end of the tent to another, arguing about how it should be done. It was the woman who'd been cursing him the day we arrived. They had a little cook fire going outside by then so I took off my socks and shoes and put them nearby, hoping they would dry. "Where's your people?" the woman asked, walking past me with a box. "I'm Nan, by the way."

"My mom's Laureen," I said, as though that explained everything. She shrugged, not impressed, I guess.

Skinny came over just then and sat down beside me. "Hi again," he said, and lit a cigarette.

Laughing Eyes, I thought to call him. He was like a dolphin with its fixed, perpetually blissed out smile, or those dogs with turned up lips: happy looking, even when they've just been kicked. Later, I was to come back to that observation and ponder it some more, but at the moment I was busy noticing that Skinny's teeth were white. You notice good teeth now that they're becoming rare.

"So, Camden," he asked, "you want to come check in yet?"

"Where?" I asked.

He pointed to a big orange nylon tent set discreetly back among the pines. He'd worn a path through the muck and pine needles and bits of snow. "My office," he said, a little proudly. The flap was open and inside I could see the screen of a laptop opened on a card table.

"Who set up the Wi-Fi if Laureen wasn't here?" I asked.

"Daniel can manage a local area network," Skinny said. "But there's no internet yet. We've all been waiting for your mom on account of that."

"Take her twenty minutes at the outside," I said. Skinny wasn't the sort you could complain about Laureen to, I got the feeling, so I might as well join the bragging club. Unlike some people, I had the right to.

Skinny laughed. He ducked into the tent and started typing without even pulling up his little folding chair.

"Can I wait?" I asked. "Don't feel like moving yet."

"Sure," Skinny said. "Wait for your socks to dry. Where's your boots, anyway?"

"Truck, I think," I said. "It's a bit of a mess."

Skinny nodded as if he knew all about keeping your belongings in messy trucks. "So," he asked, "you ever been to a Tribe thing before?"

"I've been to six or seven things like this with Laureen, but I've never heard of this Tribe before. If it's so important, how come she's never mentioned it?"

"Saving the best for last, is my guess. And the first. Tribe gatherings were the first, are the biggest, have always been the best. Everything else is a cheap imitation. I'm not complaining; you can't have too many these days. I'm an elitist in my own way, I suppose. Estevan is Tribe too," Skinny said. "Maybe you just haven't been listening."

It seemed possible. "But not Peter?" I asked.

"If Peter was Tribe I'd withdraw my membership," Skinny said.

"Ditto," I agreed. "Where do those crates of fresh vegetables come from?" I asked, pointing at the kitchen area that had miraculously sprouted crates and boxes of produce to augment the copious supply of cans and burlap-bagged dry beans.

"An organic farm near Redding. We make weekly runs."

"That is organized. These Tribe people must be smarter than they look." I made my own elitist face, scowling at Nan who was still muttering and moving boxes.

"Or is that part of their smartness," Skinny asked, "that they don't look it?"

As if I cared about his cryptic quips. I stared sulkily at the dripping trees.

"Forget it," he said, "whatever it is. Come for a walk?"

He was pretty cute so I said okay.

I put my still damp footwear back on. A muddy trail through pines opened onto another sloping meadow, this one empty except for a pile of logs on a rise, up out of the mud. Skinny possessively opened an aluminum toolbox sitting up on the logs, took out a thermos. He poured coffee, drank a big swallow, passed me the cup. I looked at him, weighing again. How germy could this guy be? The coffee smelled like ransoming my brain back from Laureen's second-hand marijuana smoke; I drank. We sat down, passed the cup back and forth, listening to new arrivals call to each other from far away at the bottom of the woods. The sun rose over the treetops, began burning the mist off the meadow. I took off my still wet shoes and socks, stretched out, and stared up at the sky. I heard Skinny's footsteps departing as I drifted off but when I woke up he was back, with two plates of toast and eggs. I began to cry. Skinny watched; smiling sympathetically, only a little confused. He started shovelling food into his mouth.

"You slept for three hours," he said after he swallowed. "Eat up. You're probably starving if you've been on the road with Laureen. I'll bet she's forgotten how hungry kids get."

I'm not a kid, I was going to say, but didn't, wondering how old he was. "That must be it," I said instead, wanting to apologize for coming apart, but he stopped me before I could begin. "Cry as much as you want," he said. "What the hell d'you think you came to this mountain for?" He said it like it was just a little funny, and I started to laugh. I was afraid the laughter would flip into hysteria, tears again, and Skinny said, not unkindly, "Shut up and eat."

And maybe that was all it was: nervous exhaustion and hunger and sleep deprivation and trying to get Laureen to talk about Peter.

"Why are you hanging out with me, Skinny?" I asked when half my plate was gone, vestiges of my bad mood remaining in spite of catch-up food and catch-up sleep. Maybe I needed more of each.

He stared at me. "Something wrong with you?"

"What?"

"You spit on company? I have to eat with someone; you're new, I thought we could chat. You're Laureen's daughter; I've heard a lot about you."

"That's just it. You should be in your tent, having it on with Laureen."

He choked on his food, he was so incredulous. "Laureen's never been my lover," he said. "She's twenty years older than me, at least. I just know her from, you know, Estevan's school."

"Just checking," I said, but I could tell I'd offended him. Truth is, my mom has been known to have young lovers, although Skinny would probably be breaking the half-your-age-plus-seven rule. Unlike my dad, she waited till after they split up. Maybe it was a revenge thing, or maybe, once she got older, she noticed younger guys weren't as ageist.

"You might think I bring breakfast to everyone, Camden Town, but I don't. I'm too busy." He picked up our empty plates and walked away, disappearing on the woods trail.

I sat, watching him go.

4

BROWN AND WHITE and blue: the colours of spring before the snow melts. As always, the media fast made everything seem flat and dull. I knew from experience this would pass, that in a day or two nature would seem a better content provider than my phone ever did. I was tempted to sneak into Skinny's tent and update my status on his laptop, that is, if my mom would stop moping and get the linkup finished. Anyway, what would I say? I couldn't post a link to this gathering, because there isn't one. It's intentionally all word of mouth.

Before we left Toronto, Peter said he'd come up from San Francisco and hang out, but he never did, at least not yet. We're out of range of microwave towers up here, so Laureen set up an email thing via packet radio; it's one of her specialties, basically Ham with terminals. It seemed like everyone my mother ever knew in San Francisco was saying hello, but not her old boyfriend. I, for one, didn't want to see Peter at all; the guy gave me hives when he was within a hundred feet of me.

Daniel swaggered through camp like he set up the transceiver alone, and lots of people think he did, because he couldn't be bothered letting people know.

When Skinny pointed this out Daniel had the nerve to ask what the point was anyhow—it wasn't like the drive to town was longer than half an hour.

"She was just showing off," he said. "More or less her reputation, that. And we could just as easily have built a bridge for Wi-Fi, boost the signal so it gets up this far from town."

Talk about pivoting.

"Everyone knows Wi-Fi is bad for you," Skinny said sagely.

"Nice, Daniel," Laureen said, overhearing. "Did it ever occur to you I'm going to run a workshop showing everyone how I did it? Useful skills they might be needing somewhere, some time. Even you."

"Not just that," I said. It was a little unnerving the way everyone looked at me to hear what I was going to say next. Usually when I'm standing in a group chatting, even outside, we're all looking at our phones while we talk.

"What?" Daniel asked, staring down at me from under his eyebrows, too bushy by half.

"Not everyone has a car. Not everyone wants to beg rides. There's people without phones. Speaking as a non driver."

Laureen gave me the biggest grin and I almost wished I complimented her in public more often. Almost.

I extricated myself since I didn't have a phone to get out and stare at, wandered off after a half-hearted wave goodbye. Most people here were my mom's age, either that or they were around thirty, trailing little kids and carrying babies. There was no one to talk to, no one close to my age other than Skinny and he was busy, running up and down the mountain doing his Security thing, wearing the same white T-shirt and a plastic police hat that suited him. I was bored.

5

DAY SIX. "Here's a little cash," Laureen said this morning, pulling a red Canadian fifty dollar bill from the duct-taped billfold she kept in the pocket of her old down vest. "Not that you'll need it; I'll only be gone overnight. There's nothing to buy here anyway."

"Tie-dye T-shirts over there," I pointed.

After breakfast, the picnic tables outside Kitchen were often used to display dried herbs, hand-screened T-shirts, 'zines, and beaded earrings: more clutter to fill your pack with.

Laureen rolled her eyes.

"No, some of them are nice," I said.

"You need more shirts, really?" she asked, digging in her other vest pocket where I knew she kept her pipe.

It's always a climate adjustment going from one parent to another. Lark will say, "You're bored? Go to the mall with Kaylee. Here's twenty bucks. Bye."

Laureen is just the opposite. She gave me a put upon quizzical look and asked, "Did you forget to bring clothes?"

My mother really doesn't understand why anyone would buy a piece of clothing if they didn't have to. She also looked a little guilty, as if I was going off to school with no clothes on at all because she'd somehow forgotten to provide for me. Which was a look I'd seen a lot of too.

I would've rolled my eyes right back at her and made a smart remark, but she was leaving. I didn't actually see her go, later that morning. She told Skinny to tell me she'd be right back, which was what she'd told me, too. Something about her saying it so often worried me a little.

But a day was a day was a day, right?

6

WHAT IS IT ABOUT your parents walking out of your life, over and over and over? Lark did it first, with the first model. Now he does it by sending me to the mall with credit cards. Laureen just does it, climbing into her truck and going. Mostly she asks me if I want to come along; I have to give her that. I usually say no, preferring my father's absenteeism, his plastic. This time I actually would have gone with her down to San Francisco just to get away from the muck, but she never asked.

We were at the log pile in the second meadow drinking coffee when Skinny told me the reason she'd left wasn't just to look for a part she needed, but to pick up Peter, her old beau I'd never liked.

"Peter. All I need," I said.

"Have you ever noticed how hardware geeks can't read people very well?"

"My guess it's partly why my mom became a hardware geek," I said. "Low on social skills, she needed to develop expertise in another area."

Skinny laughed so hard he spilled his tin cup of coffee and almost fell off our log pile. When I think back, he laughed too hard for what I said.

"I remember the first time they met," I said once he'd stabilized. "We were driving down from British Columbia and picked Peter up hitch-hiking. I must have been nine or ten; my parents had already split up. He was on his way from Seattle to meet up with an activist puppet theatre in Oakland. My mother's always liked thespians, although she's on the science side herself. Amazingly, they're still together off and on. Thing is, I didn't really like him, even when I first set eyes on him."

"Unlike your mom, you read people well," Skinny said.

I wondered about that. My mother and Skinny seemed good friends, but I had the feeling Lark would've distrusted his homemade tattoos, just for starters. My dad was an actual honest to god rock star, albeit a minor one, but the rebel often seemed long gone in him, if it had ever existed.

"Including you?" I asked.

Skinny shrugged and I worried I'd offended him again. He tapped the ash from his hand-rolled cigarette and rubbed it into his black jeans.

"Is that to keep bugs away or what?" I asked. Like Daniel and my mom and Nan and other Tribe folks, Skinny was up on outdoor survival skills. But he was staring at me kind of vacantly and I wondered whether he'd even heard what I said.

"Where are you?" I asked.

"Sorry, I was dissociating."

"So it seemed. Anyway, I told Laureen what I thought."

"What'd she say?" he asked.

"She said I was just jealous of the attention she was paying Peter instead of me. Now that I'm older I still think I was right. It's not like he didn't try and charm me, at least at the beginning. It just didn't work on me the way it worked on her. I'm my father's daughter. I've got a few performer's genes myself so I can smell a player."

"Takes one to know one," Skinny agreed. "Unlike Laureen, who's shy as they come, kind of Aspie really." He picked up a lump of soggy snow from a patch of shade and rubbed it between his hands. When he was done he opened them and looked, nodding in satisfaction at their newfound cleanliness.

"Yeah. Also unlike Laureen, I can usually smell it when people are acting." I examined my own hands. There weren't too dirty and there were only tiny flecks of pale blue polish remaining on my nails, unfortunately stuck to the cuticles. My friend Kaylee would've had fits, wheedled someone into driving her down the mountain to the store just so she could buy Cutex. "It pissed Peter off when I didn't warm up to him," I told Skinny. "More than a little."

Skinny leaned forward then and hugged me, right out of the blue. It was strange because he's not a very touchy guy, in spite of the big hug he gave my mom when we first arrived. Then he abruptly got up and walked away down the trail back towards Kitchen, mumbling about some files he had to update, not meeting my eyes.

Later he told me it was because he was crying, but it was a long time later.

7

DAY SEVEN. Some new teenagers have shown up, in couples or threes or all alone, hitching from one city or little town or another. They're not Tribe teenagers. They stick to themselves in little campsites far back in the woods, or right out in the open near Kitchen, where you're not really supposed to camp. Maybe they're afraid of bears and think the presence of large quantities of canned goods might keep them safe.

Free food. The great outdoors. We have variations of the same weird conversation. It's happened a few times now, crossing paths with new kids wandering through muddy meadows. Sometimes they're in rags that make me ashamed of my fancy jeans and new Reeboks, admittedly mud-covered by now. I know for some of them the rags might be part of their look but even so, I still put mascara on first thing in the morning, don't ask me why. I do it looking in a piece of broken mirror someone balanced between two nails on one of the posts holding up the new sun and rain shelter Skinny and Daniel built over the picnic tables outside Kitchen.

"Are your parents here?" I asked a girl I met there this morning. She looked haggard and wet and hungry; shamefacedly asking for coffee as if she might be refused. I elbowed Nan away from the big urn she was acting like she owned and poured the girl the biggest mug I could find.

"I'm here alone," the girl said in what I guessed was a French Canadian accent that made her, like me, pretty far away from home. A whole continent, almost.

"*J'ai besoin d'un café aussi*," I said, pouring myself one in the second largest of our small hoard of mainly chipped ceramic mugs. She laughed but it was a nice laugh and I think she appreciated my trying. As lost as I sometimes felt, I still had an in compared to her, knowing Skinny and being related to Laureen.

Not that Laureen was here. And when she was, she didn't toot her own horn very much, in spite of her legend.

Nan glared at us, imperiously sweeping her long black hair over the cutting board where she was about to get to work with what looked like a good knife and a bushel of potatoes. Yuck.

"She brought me here and left," the girl said.

I wasn't sure I should ask who *she* was. But after I thought about that, I realized we weren't so different. "Know the feeling," I said.

"She heard this was a place," the French girl said. Between gulps she stared at her coffee as if it was liquid gold, as if she'd forgotten such a thing could exist but had missed it nonetheless.

"A place?" I asked.

"What?" she asked.

Why did everyone here dissociate so much? Was it something in the water? Or was it our minds evolving, as I'd overheard Nan say? Or maybe it was the Lemurians from Telos, their city inside the mountain, trying to communicate with us.

"She heard this was a place," I said. "What kind of place?"

The girl thought for a minute, trying to retrieve the memory. "A place you can come."

I nodded. "How old are you?" I asked, trying to figure out

if I was still the youngest adult here. If you can call a teenager an adult. If they have no one to look after them then what else can you call them?

"I'm seventeen," she said, wiping away the dark hair plastered over one eye by the eternal morning rain. "But I left two years ago. And then I went back, just to visit. I missed her, even after everything what happened." She gulped her coffee, gratefully.

"The food police on Kitchen Committee must have lightened up a little," I said.

"Why?" the girl asked.

"Last week you couldn't find anything but herbal tea and juice."

"Only some juices," the girl said.

"Non-acidic," I agreed.

"Yep. OJ would get you kicked off," she said and we both laughed.

Progress.

"She'll be back," I said. "I know she will." I gave the girl the biggest hug to go with the biggest mug. I remembered the hug Skinny gave me yesterday and thought maybe I was passing it on, that hugs could somehow be contagious. It felt so good when she hugged me back, hard. When the hug was done, I walked away carrying my coffee. I was grateful for the rain as it would hide my sudden unexpected tears.

Laureen hadn't returned as she'd promised she would. The day wasn't over yet, but still.

"*Je m'appelle Marie*," the girl called after me, a little reproachful.

On top of being a great hugger, Marie remembered more of her manners than I remembered of mine. First thing to go, after nail polish.

8

DAY EIGHT. And now, so quickly, I have not quite nothing:
1) Too small black rubber boots that belong to Laureen, 'cause we couldn't find mine in the truck box before she left for San Francisco to find Peter. Happy Trails, Mother. I bumped into Skinny today by the orange Security tent, asked for news; there hasn't been any. No need for worry, he reminded me. She promised him she'd be back inside three days, which means tomorrow.

2) Leather jacket. It belongs to Skinny, who I've never seen wearing anything other than his filthy white T-shirt, even on the coldest nights. Is he real? I check his skinny arms for goose bumps, see none.

3) I have my sleeping bag.

4) Our tent.

5) My name-brand phone. Which does not work up here.

9

DAY NINE. Laureen has not returned. Skinny, busy with committees, chats with me briefly to say I should take classes to pass the time. This gathering is ostensibly a healing festival; there are half a dozen different workshops under the grove of Ponderosas every afternoon, but I don't sign up for any. Parentless, and without last night's television to discuss, it seems, like my mom, I'm a shy person. I hardly speak to anyone, except for the simplest of informational exchanges, as in: Where are the latrines? On the far side of the meadow, downstream from the spring. Where do you wash your clothes? On rocks downstream, or we drive into town to the coin wash.

I do not go to the coin wash: I have no coins, no vehicle, no driver's licence, although a ride could be begged, pretty easily. Why didn't Laureen leave me more than fifty dollars? Our ration of the common food plus unlimited workshop passes are the larger part of her technician fee. Maybe she figured adding to my collection of T-shirts and beads could wait till she got back, or else she's trying to wean me of my consumptive habits.

It's true there isn't much need for cash here, as I haven't broken my bill. I could, for laundry money, I guess. And buy pop and a hamburger while I'm in town.

Remember pop? Remember hamburgers?

I'd still have forty dollars left.
I decide to hold onto my fifty.
You never know.

10

DAY TEN. No Laureen. I surreptitiously used a little of the big boxes of biodegradable laundry detergent someone left beside the aptly named Laundry Rocks. For all I know some Tribe person left them there, to deter newbies from washing their underwear with Tide back at the spring. Even I know better than that.

I guess Mom taught me more than she thought she did.

If she doesn't come back tomorrow, I'll email Lark and ask him what to do. I'll probably get an automated reply. Out of office.

Or I'll grab a ride from Daniel or someone to town.

Drink pop. Eat hamburgers. Go to the coin wash. Charge my phone while I'm there. Call Lark. Call my mom.

The coin wash in Shasta City, the little town on the flank of the mountain, looms large as a venue of possibilities. The last bastion and all that. Question: If the coin wash represents civilization, what do we represent?

Think hard, Amethyst. Just because you heard the word anarcho-syndicalism in the coffee line-up yesterday doesn't mean you (or for that matter anyone else here) actually knows what it means.

Mom's boots are handy when I want my runners to dry out, even if they are a size too small. Tight dry footwear, I've learned, can be better than roomy but wet.

Truthfully, I squelch through the mud in bare feet a lot, although Skinny points out this is a bit of a health hazard. Staph infection and all that.

Gross. I'll try and remember.

11

DAY ELEVEN. Daniel said he'd go to San Francisco to look for Laureen. He thinks I should stay, learn something, not fly east on wired airfare at the first glitch. He knows Peter's address, as well as a lot of my mother's other Bay Area acquaintances. He told me not to worry, that it was probably just truck trouble, which of course doesn't explain why she hasn't emailed. He didn't mention that and neither did I. I wasn't sure if his worry made me feel better or worse. He left this morning, and I can actually hardly wait to see my mother. I also gave him Lark's email and told him to write—ask whether he'd heard from Laureen. Just in case my mom's packet radio setup is being glitchy.

I guess you have to develop a sense of humour.

More people arrive every day, are as thrilled as the others to:

1) Dig more desperately needed latrines.

2) Help each other push their vehicles out of the mud.

3) Hang their damp sleeping bags on lines strung between trees every morning.

4) Build tipis and lodges out of the Lodgepole Pines, in which yet more healing workshops will take place.

5) Build saunas over the runoff, for healing and getting clean.

Really, I ought to take one. Thank God the little mirror in Kitchen disappeared.

12

DAY TWELVE. Chatting with Skinny over breakfast I made a sarcastic remark about all this healing. Loud enough to offend anyone who was inclined that way, he said, "For instance, abuse survivors have a couple of crappy choices. Number one, suicide, or they can unload their pain by passing it on to the next generation."

"What's wrong with therapy?" I asked, wondering at his lack of irony. I couldn't read his motivation. Was he trying to shock me or was he just being a jerk? Everybody gets to be a jerk sometimes, but from what I'd seen of Skinny, he indulged less than most.

He got up abruptly to collect empty and half-empty oatmeal bowls to take to Kitchen where Nan was busy building up the fire so she could boil water.

"Sure," he agreed, coming back for more dishes, "And crystal healing and Lomilomi and steam-filled lodges. And political theory. They all help too."

He looked at the picnic bench as if he was wondering whether to sit back down or not. I patted it. Reassuringly, I hoped.

"Busted," he said, but sat facing out so he could make a quick escape if he needed one. "How do we create something new from the ground up? If you could create a world, if you had that power, what would it be like? That's why we're here, isn't it? So we can ask and try to answer that question?"

"Nah," I said, watching him fish rolling papers and a little pouch of tobacco out of his back pocket, and begin rolling himself a cigarette. "The new kids here aren't asking anything like that. A French Canadian girl I met in the coffee line-up said she was here because she'd heard it was a place you can come."

"A place you can come," Skinny said. "That's kind of profound."

"Now that you mention it, I guess it kind of is," I said. "I liked Marie. Sometimes I wonder about everyone here. Where did they come from? Where are they going? It would be cool to do little interviews, collect their stories, and transcribe them. I mean, I know a bit about you and Nan, but it would give me an excuse to to talk to more people."

"That's an amazing idea and I'd totally lend you an iPod to record the stories. I've still got one with charge I think. Anyhow," Skinny added, "you can't say we're operating outside of the state's purview because we have all the required permits, which are legion and complex."

Most folks had up and left already, and of those who remained quite a few scowled when Skinny lit up his cigarette. He drew long and hard, obviously well practised when it came to ignoring those sorts of glances.

"So who does the paperwork?" I asked.

"You don't know your mother at all, do you?" Skinny asked. "You just travel with her."

"And complain," I said. "I complain a lot while we travel. It's my age, apparently. She says I'll grow out of it."

"So did I answer your question?" he asked.

"Uh, which question?" I'd never really noticed before but among the usual hearts and skulls and flowers there was a flying mountain inside a purple pyramid tattooed on his left forearm. I wasn't one hundred per cent sure it was a flying mountain because it was the kind of tattoo your half-trained friend does, maybe a fellow traveller waiting with you in a train yard. Still, what it lost in finesse it gained in feeling; the flying mountain was smiling broadly. It was a nice touch.

"Anarcho-syndicalism means we're doing it without the state," Skinny said, reminding me of what we'd been talking about.

"I'd take help from the state," I said. "Especially if Siskiyou County sent someone up to clean the outhouses. Whoever's on that committee is failing big time."

"No shit," Skinny said and I groaned. "So join up," he added.

"Join up what?" I had a terrible urge to touch the smiling mountain but thought I had better not. From what I'd observed, except for hugging Laureen the day we arrived, and me a few days ago, Skinny seemed to have an aversion to touch. I wrapped one hand around the other to restrain myself.

"The outhouse detail," he said.

I stared at him. "You wouldn't do that in a million years."

"I have so. Everyone has to."

"Everyone?"

"Every committee member," Skinny said.

"Oh. You mean Tribe?"

I was briefly sure the tattooed mountain's smile was broadening as it listened to our conversation, as if it approved. The things lack of sleep will do to you.

"Yes," he said. "It breeds egalitarianism, having everyone do outhouse duty."

"And e-coli. It breeds e-coli too."

It was Skinny's turn to groan. "All the same it's good practice. What if there isn't one, next year or next month?"

"Isn't one what? Outhouse? How could that be, ever?" I asked. "Even if they all magically vanished you could just dig a new one."

"Isn't a state," Skinny said, squinting at me from under his silly plastic hat, which, on him, was bizarrely attractive. On some few lucky people, any hat at all just looks really good.

"Never thought of that."

"What did your mother talk about over dinner, then?"

"I live with Lark, mainly," I said. Feeling exposed, I reflexively dug in my jeans pocket for my phone. I could peer at that while Skinny peered at me. It was still there. In spite of being out of charge and out of range.

"Ah yes, Mr. Moneybags," Skinny said, getting up.

"He's nice!" I insisted. "And not rich."

"Well, it wouldn't hurt to start, Camden Town."

"Start what?"

"Healing." He looked at me oddly and walked into the woods, back down the little trail towards the orange Security tent where, I assumed, he intended to update the registration files on his laptop. A few minutes later he returned, took our dirty plates and carried them to Kitchen, which made me laugh but I thought it was cool too.

13

SEEDS

Amanda Jenkins' story, as told to Camden O'Connor

I don't know how it is I came to have no parents and no name. I heard this is a place you can come, if you lookin' for a name. I have nothing. But I have had nothing before, and now I am glad to be free of it.

Where was I before I came here? In the city. There were five of us, or maybe ten or thirty. The building was an empty one, gutted by fire. We slept on the floors, on found mattresses. I sprayed them all with a can of bug juice I bought. I do not like fleas or bedbugs.

I planted flowers. I dug the earth out of the central courtyard. An empty yard. Probably it was full of lead, but eventually that too will be washed away by rain. The rain is cleaner now.

When I arrived, there was no one there. Soon there were sometimes ten, sometimes twenty of us.

I planted sunflowers in the yard. I stayed long enough to see their big heads turn, slowly, throughout the day.

I made window boxes out of some panelling ripped out of a wall. In them I planted geraniums, herbs, and tomatoes. The seeds were seeds I brought from the East. The soil was not good, soil dug out of the yard. It was not really a yard, maybe used for parking before. One day I woke up and there were chickens in it. Where did the chickens come from? It didn't matter. They laid eggs, and I knew they would be good to eat, when winter came.

I gathered the chicken dung and diluted it with water, and carefully poured it into the pots of plants. The tomatoes did fine. When someone new came, I made them eat tomatoes. "Vitamin C," I said. They looked at me strange; their eyes wide and dark, blank as stones. "Eat your tomatoes," I said. They were young, most of them. They were young and frightened and ready to fight, and yet their mouths were all open, as though they were expecting something wonderful to come out of nowhere, to fly in. They gathered from the edges of the burnt city, hearing. What did they hear? That there was a place, a place you could come. My sadness was that I was alone, that I was older than everyone there, that I had to look after them all. They played with each other, giggling and combing one another's hair. They were like children, really. They ran up and down the halls of the building, delighted, discovering things. Exploring. They liked to rearrange, to take things apart and rearrange them. I remembered, I did that too. It was necessary, if they were to learn. Why we were here and not somewhere else.

I looked after the plants and made the children eat them. I hoped that none of them would get sick with something I could not cure. I made them eat garlic and drink tea brewed from nettles and burdock root. So they would be strong, would not get sick. I dreamt of someone coming over the hill. A man. He would arrive soon, I dreamt. He would help me in my work. I did not mind after a time, being always alone, being lonely. I no longer looked for anyone to fall into, to carry me. I made the youngsters drink their teas. I made them wash. I watched as they played their secret, whispering games. I did not mind anymore. I didn't mind not being one of them, but one of the others. The man coming over the hill. I realized he wasn't coming over the hill, but was one of the ones here. He said his name was Stephen. He was maybe nineteen. He was very strong. I leant out the window, watching him. He was leading the children. "Shit in the pit," he said, "not in the sunflowers. Wash your hands before you eat. Here, drink this tea." He yelled at them sometimes but they did not really mind. As he became stronger, I disappeared into the shadows. I lurked in the hallways, disappearing. I could because there wasn't so much responsibility; now someone had grown, like a sunflower ... he was almost ready to harvest for seed. Ready to be an adult, come to help me shoulder the weight. I was glad. He did not speak to me, Stephen, but I could hear his voice in my mind, asking questions. I answered, from my room hidden in the dim corridors.

Yes, you can do this and this and this. Yes, the windmill on the roof is good. They will help you. You must make them work, teach them it is important. Energy and power. Their own. At first they won't believe you, will not understand why, just as you did not understand, thought it was enough just to drift, to be asleep to your own power. Yes, you can do it. You can.

"Will you help?" he asked me in my mind. "Yes," I said, "I will." After a time they could hardly see me anymore. Stephen saw me, but only dimly, like something half forgotten, like a dream. He had already forgotten that I used to be a real person. He had forgotten I used to be flesh and blood like him, that I too suffered, hated to be so alone. I watched him cry, alone, sometimes at night. I cannot do it, he cried, calling out my name. I cannot do it, I cannot. You must help me. You say you love me, so you must help. You don't know what it's like to work so hard for so little. Everything is darkness here, and I cannot see.

"You can see," I said. "There is a little light inside you, and if you turn it on, you will see everything, everything." He did then, at first tentatively, like an experiment, and then the whole yard was shining, illuminated, and he could see the faces of the children, some sleeping, some waking. They could not see his light, but they knew something had changed. They stirred in their sleep, smiling, cuddling one another.

"You aren't a human being," he said. "You cannot know how it hurts."

"Oh?" I said, but my heart hurt for him, for his hurt. Then he was better again, and happy. How I loved him. One day I will go back for him, and then we will be together. At night, when they were all sleeping, I made the rounds of all my window boxes, gathering seeds. Seeds from tomatoes, from echinacea, cucumber, geranium, hyssop, basil. Parsley, horsetail, garlic. Valerian, bergamot, mint. Sunflowers, zinnia, sweet pea. And of course, the beans and corn. I dried the seeds on the roof, under the sun. Then I climbed the stairs again, at night. Up, up the stairs, all around the shadowy building, leaving it behind: its weight, its solidity. Each floor I went up I looked at the sleeping faces, blessed them all. Each floor I went up I felt a lightness, a greater freedom. On the roof there were stars. One of the stars moved and came closer. In a great swoop of the mind I was lifted up up among them. They welcomed me, princes of peace. I recognized them all. We skimmed over the night, looking for lights. Where we saw lights, we hovered and sent our minds down into their dreams, the sleeping children. They did not know we had been there, but they felt a presence, a kindness, a benevolent intent. We were happy and shining.

**

Far below I saw a girl, walking over a hill. In her knapsack she held a packet of seeds and a bottle of water. Through the canvas of the knapsack I could see the seeds, the life inside them glowing like light bulbs. And on another hill, there was a man. He was making something, a new kind of machine. One day, I knew, he would put it on the roof, and it would spin light and energy down from the stars.

THE END

14

DAY THIRTEEN. Skinny sought me out at breakfast, once again at the row of pushed together picnic tables outside Kitchen.

"I guess your mom's not back yet," he said.

"No. She left on day six, which makes it a week." I gestured for Skinny to sit down but he shook his head no.

He had the faintly jittery look he often got, as if he couldn't keep still long enough to sit down for five minutes, even beside me, who he mostly seemed to think was sort of okay for company.

"What do you do, scratch the days on the tent wall?"

"Or Daniel either," I said, ignoring that.

"Two since Daniel hasn't come back."

I scooted over to make room. While he could stand there drinking coffee and holding a bowl of oatmeal, there was no way he could eat his breakfast that way short of slurping it down.

"Sit," I said.

He smiled, gave me his coffee, and ate standing up. "Later. I'll sit with you in Second Meadow later. But I gotta go in a minute. There's been trouble in the parking lot overnight. Folks sleeping in their vehicles got in an argument about their dogs fighting."

"I miss having our truck to sleep in," I said. "Our tent fell down in the storm and when I put it back up it sagged all down one side and it leaks now. Either the tent's half dead or I'm a terrible camper, take your pick."

I didn't tell him how much I missed Laureen. I didn't want him making fun of me. In spite of his perpetually laughing eyes, there was something a bit scary in him, a little intense. I couldn't tell if it was real or for show, and I had to think about what the difference even was.

I looked up at him, noticed his hair was growing in under his hat; he had tattoos and piercings both, but all the same his vibe was a little like the orange-robed Hare Krishnas I'd seen panhandling in Vancouver or more accurately, I suppose, Zen Buddhist monks my mother knew in Toronto.

The oddest part was that, along with his menacing undertone, he had this eminently believable quality. Based on that, I'd have given him my life to look after in a second, and not only do I not trust strangers, I barely trust my parents to keep me safe.

I mean, who would?

Like Marie said, *she* brought me here and left.

Of course I knew who *she* was.

There's only ever the one, isn't there?

"What are you," I finally asked, "a punk or a monk?"

"Good one," he said, and took off to make his security rounds but half way across the meadow he turned and waved. It seemed like he was always turning back, to wave, to collect dishes, to smile, to see if I was still there. I liked it.

I sat there for a while and then thought maybe I should try and learn something after all, walked to the lower meadow where the workshops were being held. I came across a group sitting under a pine. A young woman with long red hair lay on the ground in the middle, whimpering, while the others stroked and prodded her with their fingers.

"What are you doing?" I asked, after watching for a while. A new technique, foreign sounding name, some type of deep body massage. "Kind of like reflexology," I offered when nobody answered, trying to sound in the know. "I've always wondered why there are so many kinds of bodywork. Why can't they somehow amalgamate them all under one heading? It's all energy work, right?"

Not just the guy demonstrating but everyone in the group, including the whimperer, gave me the evil eye. What they were doing wasn't like reflexology at all, apparently. And if I didn't know why there were different kinds of bodywork, I knew less than nothing.

I wondered where I'd gone wrong. You were supposed to be able to say anything at these gatherings; they were very big on free speech. I missed Skinny. I knew he would've laughed and then wondered how I knew. Maybe it was just us. Maybe right from the beginning there was a powerful current of empathy between us.

I wished my mom would come back for a new reason. If she did, I could ask her everything she knew about him.

The group leader said, "Sit down and join us, everyone gets a turn. I'm Ron, by the way." He held out his hand, accompanied by a warm smile.

I shook. "Amethyst."

"Amethyst," Ron beamed. "Beautiful name. Very soon you'll see just how advanced we are here from reflexology."

He sounded just condescending enough for all to notice and some to titter, but I sat down anyway. Making an effort, I guess.

Ron continued to demonstrate the proper technique on the same volunteer. She allowed all six members of the group to copy him, poking her soft abdominal tissues one after the other. By the third prodder her screams had died down a little. Maybe the prodding was working and she was being healed of her trauma, whatever it even was. Or maybe the prodders were learning, no longer poking her so hard or so ineptly that screaming was her only recourse.

Or maybe she had gotten tired of her own performance.

"Trauma alters your brain chemistry so the necessary amounts of serotonin for you to experience a feeling of well-being on a regular basis are no longer released," Ron told us. "The purpose of this work is to stimulate the brain centres responsible for chemical manufacture so that once again, serotonin is increased to a pre-trauma level. And sometimes heightened. It's not reversible; the change is permanent. It's more effective at altering brain chemistry than talk therapy," he droned on. "Let's face it, we're basically all suffering from Post Traumatic Stress Disorder, whether from something that happened in this life or a previous one."

"Can PTSD carry over?" the woman being prodded abruptly asked between faint cries. "We have different bodies from one life to the next. Different brains."

"True enough," Ron said. "Let's put it this way. It sure feels like it sometimes, doesn't it?"

Then it was my turn to prod. She abruptly began to scream loudly all over again.

"I'm being raped," she explained between screams, "by my uncle in China three hundred years ago."

I disengaged as politely as I could, standing up to say goodbye. Ron stepped in to take my place. The woman was still screaming by the time I reached the edge of the woods. I took a wide berth around the past life regression workshop, heading to Kitchen instead.

When you're at a loss, chop wood and carry water.

It was some famous Zen thing Laureen told me on some road trip long ago, by way of encouraging me to help with camping chores. There was no guarantee you'd feel better afterwards, but you'd have a woodpile and filled buckets. Or, in our case, aired sleeping bags, a clean frying pan, and coffee set up and ready to go in the morning. While I did all that, she'd check the oil and tires and do other car stuff I'm ashamed to say I still don't understand.

I stopped thinking about Laureen being gone while I worked, and Nan was appreciative. If Tribe was a collective, I'd wondered more than once, why was Nan always running Kitchen? I finally asked her.

"Because I can't stand other people's incompetence," she said. "It's not very egalitarian, I'm afraid."

"Plus it's way more work for you."

She shrugged.

In the evening after dinner I sat by the big fire circle, listening while people played instruments and sang, including a kid younger than me who did an only respectable rendition of "House of the Rising Sun."

"First song I ever learned," he told us when he was done.

"Yeah, like everyone else," I said, but quietly, and Skinny, who had snuck in behind me unnoticed at some point chuckled and said, "And it was never all that good to begin with."

"He's so smug," I complained. "I'll bet he's got parents."

"Pretty soon they'll be a bigger status symbol than top-tier Nike shoes."

I laughed and squeezed sideways so Skinny could sit down beside me. "I remember Lark telling me it was the first song he ever learned too. He was eleven and didn't have a clue what it meant but it still made him feel like crying. He said music gives people a chance to show feelings they don't let themselves share otherwise."

"You can't mean it heals," Skinny said.

"Not when that kid does it. God, I know how awful I sound. Maybe it's spoiled me, having Lark for a father."

"And what about Lark?" Skinny asked.

"Lark?"

"Does your father's music heal?"

"My mom said it did."

Skinny didn't seem like the type who carried a comb in his pocket but he procured one just then and gently took it to my hair.

"Ouch," I said, although it didn't hurt, not at all.

"You need it," he said. "When was the last time this hair saw a comb? You're halfway to dreadlocks."

"Uh, Tuesday? What day is this?"

Skinny didn't answer, maybe because the next guitarist was actually good, and after "Woodstock," he put his comb away and snuck off before I could stop him.

I waited for him to come back and when he didn't I got up and crept back to Kitchen, where I've been sleeping since my tent fell all the way down. It's dry on rainy nights.

In the middle of the night someone shone a flashlight in my face. I was as terrified as the time last summer when Kaylee and I got caught pool hopping by the police. But the cop hat was just Skinny's. "So this is where you sleep? I've been wondering."

"What time is it?" I asked.

"Three o'clock," he said. "Everyone's gone to bed. You awake enough to get up? I got a couple beers."

"Yeah, I'm awake enough." I sat up.

"Nice bag, man, is it a Mountain Co-op?" He toed the pile of discarded sweatshirts and coats I'd been using for covers. I'd abandoned my sleeping bag, a drenched crumpled ball under the most collapsed corner of my tent. Chopping wood and carrying water I was not.

"My mom forgot to leave me one," I lied, standing up.

"Nice going, Laureen. C'mon let's go," he said, and because I trusted him I followed, not knowing where we were going.

"She's always been absentminded," I explained, following the flish flash of his little light along the trail. "I guess it's 'cause she's so smart and her head is too full of her power projects to remember day to day details."

Skinny stopped dead in his tracks. He turned around and stared at me, a fact I could make out even in the dim light. I felt like I had on the first day, when he'd asked me what I did other than my nails. What had I even said?

I didn't want him to disappear like he usually did when I said something dumb, this time leaving me alone on a trail I didn't know, in the middle of the night, without a flashlight or even a candle in an empty pickle jar, so I blundered on, "for some stupid reason I've been too shy to ask anyone to borrow a sleeping bag."

"I see." We were walking again and then I heard the sound of a zipper. The torch flashed on orange nylon; Skinny disappeared inside the flap and came back out with a fraying but dry and clean quilt. He folded it in half and draped it around my shoulders. "You should have said something sooner. There's still a little bit of fire down at Circle, and it's nicer now that the crowds are gone."

When we got back to Circle, Skinny reached between two large boulders, took out a little soft-sided cooler, and got us each a cold Molson's.

"You have ice?" I asked. "What's with you?"

"Daniel went to town today. I asked him to pick me up some." Skinny stopped, as if he shouldn't have said anything. Daniel going to town meant Daniel had come back from San Francisco without my mother and already left again.

No one had told me. Spare the child, with the emphasis on child.

"Never mind," I said. "So, you've just got these little stash boxes everywhere, haven't you? Coffee here, beer there—where do you keep your drugs?"

"A man's got to take care of himself."

So dark I couldn't see his face although I knew that even if I could, he'd look like he was just about to laugh. Wondered too that he called himself a man. What would have to happen for me to start calling myself a woman? Wondered how old he was, who his parents were, if he had any. But I didn't ask any of that. Asked him what he wished instead.

He didn't hesitate, as though he'd been waiting for someone to come along and ask that. "I wish I could sit with them all and be so innocently healed of something that was pretty minor to start with."

"Or else was something you don't even know about," I added, "something that happened half a world away in another lifetime."

"Yeah," he agreed. "It's not even that I don't entertain the possibility of all that. But I have enough pain from this life, thank you very much."

"That's what I thought today too," I whispered.

"I know. I talked to Rocky—"

"Ron."

"Whatever the fuck his name even is. He didn't think much of you, not that you should care. But those weren't your feelings, they were mine."

"They were mine too," I said, slugging back the delicious beer. "Where'd you get it?" I asked, legal age being twenty-one in California and he didn't strike me as that old. Not only that, but alcohol was banned at the gathering. Gets in the way of healing, Nan told me. Probably true, except that Skinny and I were having a little healing moment of our own that happened to include a couple of beers. The way I figured it, we weren't cheating much, if at all.

He only said, "I like Canadian things. The beer, the lakes, the people."

"Can it really help you get better, all that screaming?" I wondered aloud. "Or is it just an indulgence? Or is that what healing is? An indulgence? Of what? And by whom?"

"Beats me," Skinny said. "More prosaically, you trust me enough to sleep in the orange tent tonight? You shouldn't be all alone at Kitchen. You could get hypothermia if the temperature drops which it's done before, even in June, this high up. And bears have been known to show up."

"Okay, but no hanky panky," I said.

"Not on your life." He said it so sombrely, not like a joke at all, as if he meant it. Which disappointed me more than a little.

15

DAY FOURTEEN. Skinny was already up and gone this morning when I woke, bathed in orange light, wondering where I was. He didn't show for breakfast but I wasn't mad, figuring our three a.m. beer for a better date than chatting at the mess table, in the presence of perennial eavesdroppers. After I ate and did four tubs of dishes, I walked the trail through the Ponderosas to our log pile in Second Meadow. I hoped he would show but he didn't. When I checked the thermos it was empty.

In the line of trees to the west I noticed a trail entrance I'd never seen before, and decided to follow it. Went into that walking trance; kilometres passing with my thoughts underfoot. I remembered this from other trips with my mother, how once the dullness of no media wears off, you start to notice things again. How there's seven thousand shades of green in a meadow, another forty-two hundred in a forest, how you can drift on contemplating that forever. And our early morning conversation still in my pocket, like a warm comforting worry stone. We'd finally gone to sleep just as it began to get light out, Skinny giving me a camping pad on the ground beside his own, and a pillow, yet.

In a high meadow I bumped into lovers on the grass, a couple who'd pitched their tent far away from the madding crowd for just this purpose. Embarrassed, I hiked still higher, found an alpine meadow with a stream running through it and so many tiny wildflowers in so many shades I had to sit and look at them for at least an hour. Kept going then, for the trail, while faint, continued. More woods, another meadow, where I stopped at old fire rocks and dug in my pocket for the film can of safety matches Skinny had given me. I found enough dry kindling to get a small fire started; enough to keep me company and something to do.

Felt more at peace. Maybe it was true that it didn't matter, any of it. Maybe I didn't need to know why I was on the mountain, what was going to happen, where my mother was. It was hard to stay angry because now Laureen was gone but it still seemed strange to me that she'd want to see Peter, not after what I'd told her. Even if she didn't believe me, it was rude. And the not believing me part always made me crazy.

But maybe it was enough, just to be on the mountain. It didn't rain every day and in the heat the earth even dried out sometimes.

I fell asleep, thinking maybe it wasn't answers I needed after all. I dreamt Skinny and I were making love.

16

Day sixteen. Late June. It got cold if not frosty. I've been going for my long solitary walks wearing clothes that belong to others. Still chilly in spite of Skinny's jacket and a ratty shawl I found in the goodwill box.

Most of the kids younger than fifteen came with an adult, although there's a handful of twelve- and thirteen-year-olds here all on their lonesome. So, while I'm worried about Laureen, it also makes me feel spoiled to complain about it. Unlike some, I did have a mother until quite recently. And I still have her; I just don't know where she is. And Lark is in Toronto where I left him, although he hasn't answered my emails. I've slept in the orange tent every night since I was first invited, but Skinny hasn't touched me, not once. At first I thought this was good, meant he is good, but now I'm not sure. I know many of the teenagers here are having it on with each other. Free condoms. Get yours now! A big box discreetly brought out at Circle Rock, every evening at campfire time. More fun than Girl Scouts!

Wrote to Lark again today.

"Why don't you come to Shasta, write him yourself? Just in case your mom's system is wonky? With all due respect."

Daniel's biker demeanour has always put me off but he's softer with me than he used to be, or else I'm finally getting used to him. I know it's partly how unkempt he is and that where I come from, or rather where my dad comes from, people clean themselves up. Maybe I'm judging by appearance less than when I got here, just over two weeks ago. Is that how long that takes?

"If he hasn't written back to your address, why would he write to mine? You're getting mail, right? It's not like your email's dead?"

He shook his head, stuffing his phone back in his pocket. Then he got it out again.

"Write Laureen?"

"Uh, yeah. Okay. But you've been writing her?" I looked at my feet. What had possessed me to buy white Reeboks? And my jacket. It was a turquoise Patagonia, made out of recycled pop-bottles or Goretex or something that I still wore when it wasn't so cold I needed Skinny's leather. The mud was ground in so deep it would never come out, no matter how many times I sent it to the cleaner's. If there still were cleaners.

He nodded. "And texting. But you're her daughter. I mean, if anything, you know, was weird, she'd be in touch with you more than me. Because of that."

"Uh, okay. It's not like I haven't been writing her."

"I know. Just in case, like we said." He passed me the phone.

What should I say?

Daniel looked flummoxed and turned his back.

Hey Laureen, I miss you. Where the fuck are you? Sorry for swearing. I don't usually swear. I know you do, but Lark doesn't like it, so normally I don't. I know you don't care. I wish you were here.

I thought about erasing it. I was babbling, my nerves shot. I left it. What mattered was making contact, not what I said or didn't say.

I love you. I hope you didn't disappear because I burned the food too often, ha ha.

All my love, Amethyst.

PS: *I still have all the money you gave me. I work in Kitchen a lot. Me and Skinny and Nan. I've gotten to know them both. You have nice friends.*

"Okay," I said.

Daniel turned around and took the phone back. He hadn't wanted me to think he was spying while I wrote. I started choking up. That was why I hadn't asked to go to Shasta with him. I needed a little distance. Not just from her disappearance, but what it was doing to me. The overwhelm. Denial can be a survival tactic.

"I'm sorry," he said. "I'll go back to SF."

"What happened when you went?"

"Nothing. There was no one there, at Peter's. No Peter, no Laureen. I went three times a day for three days. I called and texted and wrote them both all the time. Then I left."

"It's weird my dad isn't writing back."

"Come with me to Shasta next time."

"Or I can give you his phone numbers." I was asking a lot, I knew. "You don't have to call, you can text."

"We'll see. I'll let you know before I go again. By then you might have changed your mind."

17

DAY EIGHTEEN. No Skinny at breakfast. I helped with dishes after, and then went to Kitchen and chopped carrots for Nan's carrot lentil soup. She makes it with wild ginger from the forest and it's better than anything.

That was where Skinny found me.

Nan heaved a damp cardboard box up onto the table in front of him by way of greeting. Halfway there the bottom gave way and then there were piles of carrots in the dirt. I started picking them up.

"Why don't you be a grownup and help?" she asked him.

"I don't ever want to grow up," Skinny said.

Nan rolled her eyes and bent for carrots.

"I thought I heard you say you're a man," I said. I didn't expect him to say that men weren't kitchen slaves or anything dumb ass like that because he's not the type, but I was curious. Maybe he was being a jerk just for fun again.

"There's a difference between a man and a grownup," he said, and changed the subject. "A friend of Estevan's told me one of the things they did at EST to help you let go was get you all in a room shitting together."

"They can do that here, too, only it's a lot cheaper," Nan laughed, and put a knife and cutting board in front of him. Obediently, he began to chop.

"My point exactly," he said.

"Excuse me?" If there had been a workshop on group poos I'd missed it.

"Have you seen the four-seater outhouse with no dividers?"

"I have," I said, not pointing out I hadn't used it when anyone else was. "Somebody's idea of a joke?"

"Me and Daniel just ran out of wood. I think now people dare each other to use it, to show how tough they are. Not intimidated by bodily functions and all that," Skinny said.

"What's EST?" I asked.

"One of those expensive white guy guru things that were popular back in the seventies and eighties," Skinny said. "Turned out Erhard was abusive."

"You know, the usual crap," Nan said.

I didn't know, really, but didn't want to draw attention.

Now that she had two captive choppers, Nan took her whetstones out of the leather tool bag she always wore and began sharpening knives.

"Have you ever been raped?" Skinny asked.

Did he mean me, or both of us? It seemed like he'd asked the room at large.

Nan went first. "Not technically," she said. "A boyfriend of my mother's used to try and feel me up, and it got pretty gruesome on one or two occasions."

"I'm sorry, Nan," Skinny said.

"It was a long time ago," she said, wiping the oil off her large and now very sharp knife. "I'm a different person." She glanced at Skinny. "A grownup. I wouldn't let anyone fuck with me now. That was the lesson."

"Hard lesson for a twelve-year-old," Skinny said.

"Harder for an eleven-year-old," she said.

"No doubt. You?" he asked me.

"Ditto. Nan exactly, weirdly enough."

They both laughed as if that was the funniest thing they'd

heard in a long time. I didn't quite get the joke and finally had to ask.

"The commonality," Nan said. "In more than one sense of the word."

"One of my mom's boyfriends molested me," I said. "He rubbed her feet in sweet almond oil when she was exhausted. He made her laugh. She didn't know he'd come over when she was out and corner me. And I know there are worse kinds of child abuse than being felt up by your 'uncle' in the kitchen, but it made me furious. I wish I'd been told it was okay to say no, maybe I'd have done it sooner. Not just about that, about anything. Taught how to say no. And Laureen didn't pay much attention when I told her."

"It's the transgressive aspect that's wounding as much as anything. The violated boundary. We never recover, not entirely. No matter how much therapy," Skinny said.

"Why did it take me so long to tell him to stop?" I asked. "Why did I feel I didn't have that right? There was the surreal movie aspect to it all—it shouldn't be happening and so in one way it couldn't be."

"You're never the same, Skinny, you're right about that," Nan said. "I hated myself. First because I couldn't tell him to stop, then when I did tell him, he didn't listen, not at first anyway."

"You're lucky he did eventually. That didn't work for all of us," Skinny said.

"I was so flabbergasted," I said. "It just felt too impossible and weird, something that wasn't supposed to happen, coming from someone I was supposed to trust, someone my mother cared about."

"I know this sounds bad," Nan said, "but it's hard to imagine Laureen being dismissive. And I don't even like her all that much. Respect, yes, like, not always. I'm not doubting you, it's just a comment on her character."

"Her and Lark's breakup was bad. Maybe she was so grateful to be seeing someone who was nice to her that she waved it away. Told herself I was exaggerating, embroidering, trying to get attention, who knows."

"The human capability for denial is monstrous," Skinny said.

"Yeah, it is. I've never really forgiven her. This was supposed to be our patch-up trip, or one of them. We've had a few. We keep having the same conversation, round and round in circles."

None of us had named any names. I was going to ask why that was but then I noticed Skinny playing with something in his pocket.

"What is it?" I asked.

"A penis," Nan said.

He pulled a little pouch out from its nest in the black denim and untied it. A crystal. Not a cluster, just one long multi-faceted finger, clear as glass. He held it out.

I took it and looked through it at refracted mist and mountain, handed it back. I was afraid of dropping it. "Very clear," I said, "I hear that's supposed to be good."

"You think I'm jaded, Camden Town, but it all helps. The saunas help detoxify. Same with the wild food, full of trace minerals to reboot your brain." Skinny glanced at me briefly before continuing. "Crystals, cranial, Birkenstock shoes. Even the mountain works."

"But I do feel it, the mountain," I said timidly. "Like a dark strong rush pulling me down and up simultaneously, smelling of pine needles and snow."

He touched my arm and smiled, apologizing for an unintended slight. "I know. Me too. They probably don't, though. That's why they all talk like that. And why I'm sarcastic sometimes."

He'd never touched me before. He'd hugged me once, near the beginning, but he'd never just casually touched me like a normal person. I didn't point it out, though. I didn't want it to stop.

Nan looked from one to the other of us. She shelved the knives she'd been working on and tucked her stones back into their pouch. Smiling, she grabbed Skinny's hat and rubbed his new fuzz. He looked briefly panicked before he got hold of himself and joined in her laughter. She'd already ducked under the awning and walked away, her long skirts swirling around her untied work boots.

"Are you okay?" I asked.

He nodded, brandishing his mineral member. "It's from Coleman Mining in Arkansas. It's where the very best come from." He grinned, putting it away again. "Maybe one day I'll show you how it works."

"Yeah," I said. "Me and the other five hundred girls here."

I guess I was fishing. I'd never seen him with a girl but he didn't read as gay. He was hard to parse although we definitely had chemistry.

He got a funny look on his face. And changed the subject.

"Five hundred, nothing. Didn't you know we have thirteen hundred folks, as of today?"

"It's funny there aren't more fights," I observed. "It's a lot of people and so many of them lead such stressful lives."

"You're not including yourself?" he asked.

"It's not that I'm not; it's just that disaster is relative. And nothing really bad has happened to me."

"That's a weird thing to say," Skinny said. "You're underage, you're penniless, your parents are AWOL, you were molested as a child, what counts as bad in your universe?"

"Well, you know, worse things. My dad has money, wherever he is. I've never been beaten up. I could've grown up in Aleppo. I have you two to lean on."

"You have first world survivor guilt," Skinny said. "Anyway, to answer your first question, didn't I tell you I know Aikido? They make trouble, I can get them thrown out."

"Who does the throwing?"

"I get Daniel and a couple of his lackeys. Sometimes I help."

"The ugly biker creeps," I said.

"Don't be so mean, Camden Town," Skinny said. "We can't all be beautiful."

He couldn't have meant me, because I, most certainly, am not.

"Apologies," I said. I should've told him I loved it when he called me Camden Town but I felt too shy.

"Taken," he said. "Anyways, they're pussycats, mostly. Guys like that usually are, have you noticed? But most people take one look at them, and they leave voluntarily."

"Do you throw a lot of people out?" I asked.

"No," he said. "Folks like it here. It's safer than downtown. They want to stay. They're good."

He was so casual it freaked me out. "How long have you lived like this?" I finally asked.

"Lived like what?" he stared at me from under the plastic brim of the ridiculous hat, which he'd put back on. I was trying to read the expression in those dark eyes. As usual, I couldn't. But the dolphin lips were smiling a little more than usual. He knew what I meant. He was having me on.

"Do you have parents?" I asked.

"Estevan raised me," Skinny said. "He and his partner were my foster parents. Your mother mothered me a fair bit, when she was around. And yes, things like this are what I know."

"True for me too," I said. "Come to think of it." When I wasn't home with Lark and his plastic.

He nodded. "Every year the rest of North America gets more like the life I've known from day one."

"It hasn't been such a bad life, has it?" I asked, reaching out to touch his smiling purple mountain. He only flinched a little.

"I don't have anything to compare it to," he said and abruptly got up and left. I was finally getting used to that.

Not much of a mall rat ever, I guess. That would be one difference between us. And the parents thing.

So he's like me, or one side of me, only more so.

18

DAY NINETEEN. I'm so transparent. There's nothing in my journal entries anymore except transcriptions of our conversations.

It's not like this tells me anything I don't know.

A voice on the trail behind me. "Hey, Camden." I liked the way he said it, his gravely voice like gentlest of sandpaper on my gonads.

Do girls even have gonads? What are gonads?

He caught up with me, although he had to stay just behind; it was a single file trail. Since I couldn't see his face it was easier to say. "I'm going to have to jump you one of these nights."

"Hey," he poked me under my shoulder blade. "Patience. You never heard of it?"

I heard him light a cigarette. I turned around. He was looking at me and smiling, but he didn't say anything more and neither did I.

It reminded me of the quitting smoking workshop I'd listened in on.

What's so hard to say that you'd rather bang another nail into the coffin than say it?

19

LOOKING FOR SOFIA
a story from Carmen, as told to Camden O'Connor

Here, look at these pictures. I shouldn't be using up my battery to show you pictures, but it's not like I can call anyone from here anyway, right? This is the squat where me and Kenny and Sofia lived, back before things heated up and I ran away to San Francisco. We had a good time living there, the three of us. But we were innocent then, if I think back on it. We didn't know how much worse it could get. We didn't know we could lose even those homes made of garbage. We didn't know yet that people we knew could die. I heard Kenny was dead. But then, I was also hearing that about him when he was alive. You know people like that, who attract disaster? Sofia didn't attract disaster; she went looking. And then when it was almost on top of her, she'd duck, and come out clean. She'd laugh at us for holding our breaths. It was a game she played. She was good at it, too; I hope she's still as good at it.

I guess I came to the mountain looking for her. I've been here for three days now, and I only just realized it, that I'm looking for Sofia. It's funny, sometimes I think I see her. I see someone way across the meadow with long black hair and I think it's her. There's a split second when I tell myself it's her, tell myself she came because she could feel it, that I was here.

I catch myself thinking that all the time; if I stay here long enough, she'll know I'm here, and she'll come to meet me. Things like that used to happen to me and Sofia all the time. We used to get our periods together. I remember this one time I went to Vancouver and our rhythms got out of sync. When I came back, she'd already had her period—but she had another anyway, just so she could have it at the same time as me. That was the kind of person she was. She'd have two periods in one month just so you wouldn't have to be alone with yours. That takes a lot of heart, I figure. But she got mad. To get even, she made me clean up her place.

She lived across the street from me and Kenny then; it was back when there were still streets in that part of town, before we started up the squatters' community. Funny the things you remember about people. Like if she was here now, and she had her period, I'd know that's what I could do to make her happy. I'd clean up a space all around her, and then I'd make her some tea and a tuna salad sandwich. She told me how this one time Kenny walked in on her. It was four o'clock in the morning; she was in the kitchen, doubled over from cramps. Kenny walks in, gets himself a drink of water, says, "I'm glad I'm not a woman," and goes back to bed. It was around then she decided she didn't like him much anymore.

When I was sad, she always knew. She'd know, and she'd come and let me cry on her shoulder, for as long as I wanted.

I'm alone now; it's been that way for years. You travel, you meet people, you even live with some of them, but you're alone. Maybe people don't know how to take care of each other anymore; they don't know how to run you a bath, how to keep an eye on you so you don't get too thinned out. I'm never with anyone now—including the people I've lived with—the way I was back then, the way I was with Kenny and Sofia. Especially Sofia. But that was one of those things I didn't figure out till later. It's bad for you to live alone too long. You start seeing things, hearing things. Sometimes, I go out on the street, and I think all the people I see have rat faces. But maybe that's not so strange. I've talked to other people who see the rat faces, too. It's just a little spooky, is all.

Kenny knew her before I did. They were still lovers, even after he and I got together. It made me jealous, and so I asked him to stop, and he did. Then later, she and I got to be best friends, and Kenny got mad. We used to sleep in each other's rooms, too, sometimes, and make love, Sofia and me, but we were best friends first. You're another kind of lover when you're best friends first, but that was something Kenny couldn't get. Still, I would've been mad, too, if I was him. She used to hold my head when I was crying about what a rat he was.

I always wondered what would happen if Sofia and I lived just with each other, with no one else around to bug us. There was always some guy she liked around, or Kenny, getting mad because we were having too much fun. When Sofia laughed, there wasn't too much more I wanted in the world.

Now it's far back enough; I'm trying to figure out what was going on all those years when we lived there. For the longest time, I couldn't figure out how I'd been dumb enough to spend four years with a moron like Kenny. Then I realized that Sofia had been there the whole time, too. Oh, yeah, right. Sofia. It's weird how you can miss the really obvious things like that. It's like living in the middle of the war and not knowing, till later, that's why everything was so weird. When I left him, I lost her, too. It was almost like I could be with Sofia only if I was with Kenny at the same time. And I always wondered what it would be like if I was just with her.

Now I'm not with anyone, and when I came to the gathering, I came looking. I think if I stay here long enough, maybe she'll show up. She always could tell what I needed, like I never could with her. I never knew what she needed from me till I went back to the squat, years later, and found nobody there. Sometimes you didn't hear anything except the sounds of cars way out on the road. I'd sit and listen to the cars for hours, and then all of a sudden, I realized that some part of me thought they were driving right through me.

THE END

20

DAY TWENTY coincides with July first, Canada Day, my country in which I am not.

I wonder what sex is really like? Like everyone else in my position, I've seen enough movies and read enough books to have a pretty clear idea, but those are out of body experiences, can't be an accurate description of something so subjective and physical.

21

DAY TWENTY-ONE. "Hey Skinny," I said over breakfast.
"Yeah?"
"How come the mountain didn't do it for you?"
"What?" he asked.
"Take away your need for cigarettes. Just being here is supposed to help you clear addictions. I've heard it said."
"It's only bad for you if you think it is," he quipped. "And I smoke all natural First Nations tobacco. It's the chemicals that are bad for you, more than the tobacco."
"Do you actually believe that?"
"Yes," he said. "No. How about sometimes?"
"Sometimes is good."
"And one other thing," he said.
"Being what?"
"Maybe I carry deeper pain than you."
"Could be," I said. "Hey, Skinny."
"Yeah?"
"Did you ever get raped?"
"Several times. Between twelve and fifteen. I already told you that."
Had he? I didn't think so. He'd hinted, but that was different. I touched his arm, tentatively, as though his skin was different now. Maybe it was. Or maybe it had been all along, all those times I didn't listen. Maybe there was something fragile and

damaged under all that, that, Security. So many different ways to use that word.

"Hey, Security."

"Yeah?"

"I'm sorry," I said.

"For what? You're really attractive, Camden Town, don't get me wrong. It's not your fault I'm fucked up."

He got up and walked away. I thought of calling him back, telling him to finish his coffee, help me and Nan wash dishes, chop carrots, shell peas, go hang out on the Second Meadow log pile, anything. But I didn't.

22

DAY TWENTY-TWO. Laureen should have listened to me about Peter. I know there are far worse kinds of child abuse out there than what happened to me, but that doesn't mean I wasn't traumatized. It's hard to forgive her. And what's harder is that she went to San Francisco to look for him. Then there's what Skinny said yesterday. Did he want to talk? I couldn't tell.

"Everybody letting go of pain together?" I asked. "Isn't that a little like four-seater shitters?"

"A little," Skinny laughed.

The logs were slick from last night's rain. He offered me a hand to steady myself after I scrambled up the pile behind him. Our pile. It definitely felt like that and I liked it, scowled when anyone else came up the trail into what I thought of as our private space.

"They had to replace it with something."

"Huh?"

"Money as status," I said.

He took up the litany. "Well-paying, yet soul and people and environment destroying jobs. Since all that's mostly gone."

"Consumption to cover up the fact you're afraid no one loves you. A culture that replaces community with shopping."

"Wow, Camden! Who have you been reading?" he asked. "Political analysis isn't what I usually expect from you."

"Jostling for status because you think if you showed your vulnerability everyone would run away or worse," I continued.

He nodded. "And you might be right, too."

We both laughed. Maybe I should've touched the purple mountain instead. I'd wanted to make a window for him to talk if he wanted, but maybe laughing was better. "All those foreclosed condominiums are going to come in handy," he said. "We'll move into them, put windmills on the roofs. They're going to have to write some new laws on squatting anyway, since it seems to be the way of the future."

"Sounds fun," I said. "Looks like Estevan saw the coming thing twenty years ago."

"Looks like," Skinny agreed. "Him and your mom."

I wondered if it was Estevan who molested Skinny? If I hear that story one more time, about some big healer or guru or other form of alternative celebrity turning out to be abusive like that EST guy Erhardt, I'm going back east. I'll get a new credit card from Lark, hole up, and go online shopping for a month.

If there is online shopping anymore. Time slides by here so strangely, and things were crumbling pretty fast even before we left Toronto. Other people talk about the news, but I haven't been paying attention.

"When we leave here," Skinny said, "I'll bet you won't notice much difference anymore."

I nodded.

Where did he think I was leaving to?

Should I be thinking about that?

Easier not to. Easier to think about touching him.

And then I realized he'd said we.

And if not Estevan, then who?

What if it was my mom, for instance?

"Anyway," I added, "Maybe it's the acceptance of pain that brings the healing, as much as all the shiatsu, past-life regression, yoga, crystal healings, and colloidal silver-making demonstrations you can stuff on a mountain."

"Indeed. But don't forget the Birkenstock shoes."

I looked at his feet.

He was, indeed, wearing black Birkenstock sandals. They caused an interesting cultural frisson juxtaposed with his tattoos and piercings.

"Where are your big black boots?" I asked. He usually wore Docs.

"In my truck," he said.

"You have a truck?" I asked.

"I do. It even runs. On bio-diesel, yet. Workshop on Make-Your-Own's tomorrow. I'm helping run it. You should come."

"The poster child of the new age," I said.

"Poster child of the Cli-Apocalypse, don't you mean?"

"Same same. Where do you intend to take this truck, when this thing's over?"

"It ain't never gonna be over, Camden Town."

23

DAY TWENTY-FOUR. "Are you ready?" he asked.

"For what?"

"Today I am going to show you what healing really is." Once again, he brandished his crystal.

"Hey," I protested. "What do you think I'm sick with, anyway?"

"Of, not with. Have you ever noticed no one uses prepositions properly anymore?"

"What's a preposition?"

"You're Sick of Everything. Am I right?" he asked.

We laughed. And then he healed me. I was stretched out on a blanket he'd laid on the mostly dry ground, my eyes closed, while he moved the stone from one place to another on my body, humming a little song he made up as he went along. Funny thing was I really could feel it; it was better than Ecstasy, and more noticeable. I don't know, maybe it's just because I had such a crush on him.

"I'm thinking of taking back my original name," I said eventually. "Amethyst, the one Lark and Laureen gave me, seventeen years ago. I'm totally cured, of all my existential teenage angst or whatever is the matter with me."

"Shut up," he said, "I'm not finished," and he kept passing it over my body, and singing, too. "What's it feel like, then," he asked. "Can you describe it?"

"What's what feel like?" I asked.

"Being whole?"

"It feels like being made of purple," I said.

"Cool. So that's why they called you Amethyst, Amethyst."

I suddenly felt it from her side, how much Laureen loved me, had loved me all along. She'd just left because she felt too betrayed. Lark was the one with money so she felt he'd be able to give me a better life. Laureen's was a fierce kind of love, like a bear's. It would kill if it had to. I felt safe.

Then she was gone.

It made me sad. I wanted her to be there again, but I couldn't find her, as if she'd left not just my mind, but the world.

When I opened my eyes I saw there were other stones all over me. Some tumbled, some crystal; little stones of every hue, stones I didn't have names for, so light I hadn't felt him placing them. I closed my eyes again. It was better that way, I wasn't sure why. I could feel more.

There was one I felt him place below my collarbone. I don't mean his fingers brushing me, which they did, deliciously, or the new weight of the stone, although I felt those too. I meant it felt like a little pop.

"What happened?" he asked.

"How do you know anything happened?" I asked.

He laughed a little. "Just tell me."

"Like the stone was being passed through a subtle membrane," I said.

"Anything else?" he asked.

"It was like the stone was carrying information I needed, and I was being made aware of that."

It was hard to articulate, and not just because I was afraid I might get laughed at.

"The stone's energy was entering your vibrational field," he said nonchalantly. "You felt it. That's all."

My eyes were still screwed shut. "So why that stone? I felt that one so much. I wouldn't have believed anything about this back in Toronto, but I felt it, just as if—"

"It likes you and you like it," he said. I could hear the dolphin smile.

"Oh," I said. "What kind of stone was it?"

"Labradorite. You should carry a piece probably. Now be quiet."

"You don't have to say it." I wanted quiet then, so that I could feel more of whatever it was.

After about an hour he began removing them, carefully placing them in little cloth pouches he tucked away into a larger pouch. His best stone went back into his jeans pocket, carefully wrapped.

"Who taught you that?" I asked. "I thought Estevan's school was just for power and communications systems."

"This is a power and communications system," he said.

"You know what I mean," I said.

"Your mother," he said.

"Wow. I've gotten back missing parts of myself," I said.

"Which parts?" Skinny asked.

"The part that knows how much Laureen loves me. It was like she was here."

"Good. I have to go grab lunch before my bio-diesel workshop. You coming?"

"I think I'll just lie here for awhile staring at the sky and thinking about my mother."

24

I WISH I KNEW what happened to my mom. I went to Shasta City with Daniel and charged my phone. I emailed and texted and tried calling her and Lark a whole bunch of times but it was to no avail.

Daniel went back to San Francisco to look for her a couple more times, but she'd left no footprints and neither did Peter. Maybe they've gone to Belize or Costa Rica or Oaxaca City.

We pretty much gave up hope that we would find them anywhere, so I was surprised when I got back from hiking to see Daniel and Skinny waiting for me. I knew right away they had news, but their faces were grim. They told me about my mother.

Laureen was never coming back.

25

SECRET CAMPGROUND
Bonnie Snow, age 16, as told to Amethyst O'Connor

It's different for girls. It's like we have this big space inside us, and everyone wants it. Men, I mean. Some men. They want it because they haven't got one themselves. That's why they fuck. That's why they sent rockets out into the heavens. They want control of space. Because space is nothingness, and it's out of nothingness that everything comes. Anything comes. So if you want something, you have to have nothing first.

You asked me about Secret Campground. Secret Campground was a good place, a place you could stay without being afraid someone would come and rape you or steal all your shit, like some of the other places. Like Lunar Beach. Jesus gave me a map to it, and that's how I found it. Who was Jesus? A guy I knew back at Potter's Curve, at the mission there. The Inter-Mission, we used to call it, for a laugh. But it was a good name, too, because it was where you went when you were between places, and isn't that what inter means, between or something? It wasn't a real mission, like a religious one, it was just a thing some people put together to try and keep their shit straight. Anyway, he gave me a pineapple for my birthday. No one else gave me anything, even though they knew it was my birthday. His name was Jesus but he called himself Potter, after the place, because he'd been there longer than anyone, and, he was, like, the mayor or something, welcoming new people when they came. The name Jesus was maybe an embarrassment for him, though there's lots of Latino guys with that name; maybe he just liked to be associated. With that place, I mean.

"Aries need birthday presents," he said, pineapple in hand. And when he heard I was coming down to Oregon he drew me the map. "Secret Campground," he said. "Don't stay at Lunar Beach, that's where everybody stays. Stay at Secret Campground; it's the place for people like you." He showed me where the path was at the edge of the woods surrounding the Lunar Beach Public Campground, how the path went through the woods until you got to Secret Campground.

***

How old am I? I turned sixteen. You too? You know what it's like then, travelling around on your own as a girl. The goods and the bads. Well, Secret Campground, then. I'd hitched a ride on a private plane, 'cause somebody told me you could do that and I tried it and it worked! Like so many things that nobody tries because they think it's got to be impossible. After I left the airport, I hitchhiked to Lunar Beach and it was just like all those places. Sleazy. People doing T'ai Chi on the beach, sitting around fires in oil drums. At night hoping they wouldn't be robbed, hoping they would get laid. No safes, too, I bet. A whole family had got their tent burned down the week before I got there, I heard. Someone didn't like the homeless, or whatever. But a real family, you know what I mean? With a mum and a dad and little kids and everything. Not like beach scum at all.

Or whatever you want to call us. Them. Us. Whoever.

I was scared to stay there. Some guys said I could stay in their tent, that I'd be safer, just in case. I didn't want to get raped. But then I knew they'd put the make on me, if I stayed. I couldn't blame them really, everybody wants to get laid, just not necessarily with each other. There was this girl I met, who was staying with them, sleeping with one of the guys. Her name was Alicia. "It's not bad really," she said. It was like she didn't mind being with him, not too much. He was okay. He didn't really turn her on or anything but what the heck, it was just for a few days, and he was good at making camp fires and going into town on food missions and stuff. And when she was with him she had lower chances of getting robbed. Or raped. If you talk yourself into wanting it, then they don't have to? I mean, what's the difference, really? Sometimes they went to the food banks and sometimes they had money and went to the co-op and sometimes they got food out of the dumpsters behind hotels. "Do you like him?" she asked, meaning the other guy. He was okay looking, I guess. Blond. And he was nice to me. He really wanted me to stay with them too. With him. But they just weren't my kind of guys, you know what I mean?

I had dinner with them, pork and rice, and then I split. I didn't tell them I was going to split before I ate, just in case they had second thoughts about feeding me. She was kind of sad I was going, Alicia was. She wanted a buddy. "You splittin' on me, sister?" she asked. "Just when I was getting to know you?"

"I'm gonna stay in the woods," I said.

"Aren't you scared?"

I didn't answer because I didn't know yet. But they just weren't my kind of guys, you know?

The path was at the edge of the campground, the other side from the latrines, right where Potter's map said it was. I was amazed; I didn't think it'd be so easy. It went through the woods, evergreens mostly, I don't know what kind. I followed it for a long time, wondering if it was the wrong path. Wondering if the map was wrong, thinking it couldn't have been so easy after all. But not turning back. Then there it was. A clearing in the woods, the floor covered with pine needles. I knew I'd found it right away. Secret Campground. I felt relieved. That I wasn't scared of nature. Two paths going out from it. I checked them out right away. One went down to the beach, only it was a nice empty beach, no garbage on it. You couldn't get to it from Lunar Beach; it was cut off by bushes and slash and rocks and shit. It wasn't connected. A separate beach.

Then there was another little path, going out the other side. It went to a stream. There was a big flat rock at the edge of the stream and on the rock there was a cup and some toothpaste and a toothbrush. They looked like they'd been there a long time, like somebody had forgotten them. Also there wasn't any other sign of anyone's stuff, so I sat down on the flat rock and had a drink of water from the stream. I just kind of knew it was good, you know what I mean? And maybe Potter had told me. Or someone, that the streams around there were good. Yeah, that was probably it.

Then I just sat there for awhile, and thought about not being afraid of staying on my own in the woods. I pitched my tent, which was then just a big long piece of heavy plastic that I kind of rolled into a tube and weighed down with rocks and tied the two points up between trees with rope. That was a good tent. People used to laugh at it but I used to wake up mornings at Potter's Curve dry as a bone and people'd be swearing at their three hundred dollar tents pouring rain on them all night. They'd kind of stare at me like I was from outer space. Girls with expensive hiking boots and boyfriends to start the fire when they were feeling too wimpy from their hike.

You know the kind. I'd stare right back.

I stayed at Secret Campground for a week, and then I fell in the river, you know what I mean. I stopped trusting Gaia's gentle hand, giving you whatever you need when you need it, no more no less. God; whatever you want to call it. The thing that takes care of you. Gives you maps to Secret Campground. Free plastic. Things like that. Limpets to scrape from the rocks. Or whatever they're called. Abalone? Already I forget, although I still know what they look like, how to pry them loose, how to eat them. The important things. The names don't make you full when you're hungry. Alicia showed them to me.

No, not Alicia. Someone else. A girl. Maybe Lydia. Alicia wouldn't have known. She never believed anything unless a guy told it to her first. Lydia. I went up to her camp and it was gone. Maybe it wasn't gone, maybe she just moved it somewhere else. Or else I missed the trail. There's a few different trails up there; some of them are people trails and some of them are animal trails, and sometimes you get them mixed up. 'Cause the place I finally got to didn't look anything like Lydia's camp. Looked more like one of Winter's places. Junky. Not like Lydia's place at all.

Lydia was different. It was like she knew everything didn't have to be horrible all the time; she knew how to make sure it was different. You could be alive a different way, be high even without drugs. But that was another of those things I didn't figure out till later.

There is another path going from Secret Campground, a path I followed one day to see what was at the end of it. I followed it and that's when I met Lydia. Lydia had a camp she'd made, a camp all her own, not like Secret Campground at all, which was nice, but it was for transients too, like Lunar Beach, only in a different way. Lydia's place was in the middle of a meadow. You could see it coming from a long way back, because of the doors. She had a big wardrobe she'd picked up somewhere and brought right out into the middle of the meadow and parked there. You could get to her camp by walking around the wardrobe, of course, but she always made you go through the doors. You walked through the closet into her place, like. And there were shelves in the closet, above your head, as you walked through, where she kept some of her stuff. Sewing stuff, mostly. Cloth and buttons and needles and thread for embroidery. I tell you, walking through that closet was strange, because she'd cut the back out and on the other side there was just broad daylight, and Lydia's camp. Her camp was just three board and stump benches around a fire circle, and, further back, a kind of cave under a cliff where she hung her pots and pans and her guitar on nails, and where she slept when it rained.

Mostly she slept outside, beside her fire. And around the benches she'd planted flowers. Little rows of marigolds and something purple; I don't know what it was. And petunias. Anywhere else petunias look kind of stupid but Lydia had them out in the middle of nowhere in the middle of a meadow in a State Park. It was funny, her flowerbeds in a field of wild flowers. Like her row of pots hanging on the wall of the cliff, her rug spread on the sandy ground.

"It's Lucy's wardrobe," she said, when I walked through it.

"Who's Lucy?" I asked.

"You've got to be kidding," she said and went to her knapsack and got it out.

"Hey, this is a kid's book," I said, but Lydia said it didn't matter, just read it, so I sat down on one of her benches and started to read, there was nothing else to do. Lydia had long blonde hair she tied back with a string and she didn't wear any clothes and I asked wasn't she afraid and she said "Of what?" and I said guys raping her and she said, "I would be down where you all stay, down there at moon beach, but not up here. Up here the wolves tell me when someone bad's coming." Lydia would say things like that to you. I almost believed her until I noticed she had this big walker hound at least I think it was a walker that loved her more than anything in this world, and that would help more than a bit.

I read, because there was nothing else to do, and Lydia said "Well, if you're going to read you might as well have some supper." She disappeared around the side of the cliff and came back with some carrots that she stewed with beans and rice; funny how everyone always has beans and rice. She had a garden back there, she said.

"What do you do in winter, Lyd?" I asked.

"Oh, I upgrade the shelter there," she said, gesturing at the cave or alcove in the cliff or whatever you want to call it. "And I wear a lot of clothes to bed." I found out later that Lydia did that to everybody who came. She made them read *The Lion, the Witch and the Wardrobe* and drink tea and eat stew.

I have to tell you about her spice rack, though. While she was cooking she'd ask you whether you liked Vegit or Spike, cause it seems like most people like one or the other, not both, like coffee or tea. She'd ask because she had a rack of spices she'd picked up from different campers who'd left them behind. Salt and pepper, three Spikes, two Vegits, four basils, cumin, curry and cinnamon, one of each. Lydia had a blanket and a knife and a guitar. She gave me the guitar. "Too much stuff," she said. "You can have the guitar."

I told her I didn't know how to play so she taught me. I stayed for four days, which is apparently really a lot, and Lydia taught me "House of the Rising Sun," "Like a Rolling Stone," and another one by a women's band I really liked but forget how to play, it was too complicated. Then she told me to leave. At first I was mad she'd asked me to leave, but then I figured what the hey, I was leaving with more than I came with. I had a guitar, and I could play it. So I left. I went back to Lunar Beach, and except for the time she saved me from

Winter I saw Lydia just one more time after that, when she came down to Lunar and shared a spaghetti dinner with me.

"What are you doing?" I asked her, "I thought you never came in?"

"Oh, sure I do," she said. "I come into town once a month." She called the Lunar Beach Campground town, even though it was hardly that.

"What for?" I asked.

"For my supplies, like everybody else. You didn't see me wading through any rice paddies up there, did you? Also I got to see how all my people are doing," she said, "I got to keep an eye on my buddy Winter." They have a big bin of rice they bring down to Lunar Beach once a day to feed all the homeless people and you bring your scoop or your cup and scoop out some rice. I thought it was pretty funny that Lydia did that too, 'cause she always seemed to have so much, compared to the rest of us, but she wasn't beyond getting some free rice.

"Winter's your buddy?" I asked, having misgivings. I'd never told her about being with him, and I didn't want to think she maybe liked him.

"Sure, somebody's got to have him as a buddy, don't they, the old pussycat," and then I saw Winter with a big bushy tail like a cat, twitching.

"So what's that all about?" I asked.

"Oh, he just likes to get people all messed up," she said, laughing. "But the truth is they're messed up anyway, he's just pointing it out to them. That doesn't mean," and she eyed me levelly, "that he doesn't dig some mighty deep pits."

Truth is, I've already gotten mixed up telling this story, because the first time I stayed at Lydia's wasn't the time she gave me the guitar. That time was after Winter, when I went back up to her place for a convalescence, although I didn't know that's what it was at the time.

She helped me to get away from Winter. It was Lydia who taught me the difference. Because she was the difference. Between people like Winter and what we could have, if we weren't so fucked up looking for trouble. Like Winter is the dark side, the dark mirror of people like Lydia.

I stayed with Winter for a month. There were seven of us, five girls and two guys. He was very sexually attractive. "You're a magic girl," he said to me, the night we met, and "I am glad to be here among you good people." Everyone was passing around plates of beans. I kept noticing how much he was eating, at the same time as talking about what a shabby scene it was and how he didn't belong there; he came from a much more up-market kind of crowd. He was just passing through—you know the rap. I did notice that, but then he told me about my magic and I just watched how he glistened. He wasn't beautiful but he had a glow. The thing with girls is, they're so sexually vulnerable. Did I use that word right?

Forget it, I know I did. Like, here you are, trying to make a place for yourself in the world, and it isn't a very friendly place. I mean, you have to worry about rape and robbery and getting enough to eat and you want to be independent and still you want to have company. So you go with what looks like company, what looks like a friend, and it turns out all they were after was your space. They want control of space.

Winter wanted control of space so he could feel powerful. He would get other people, women, mostly, to give him their power, and then he would have more. He was like a black hole, one of those black hole things they have in space. He would get near you, and he would start to suck. He would suck in all your light. And once he'd sucked enough, you couldn't get away any more, just like the light that goes into those holes.

Where does it go? Do the holes ever spit the light back out? He had all these girls and boys and we'd go on food missions together and we were a family and he was like a father to us. He said he'd take care of us and we were so glad because we thought he'd given us what we'd always wanted so badly. A loving family, and somewhere to rest. He had a house even; it was further up the beach, right on the water. You could hear the waves crash at night. It was full of rattan furniture with flowered upholstery that looked out the big picture windows at the sea. There was a big pink bedroom I had all to myself, until Winter came. It didn't seem so bad. It sure beat Lunar Beach, or even Secret Campground, for that matter. You could hardly blame me. And I didn't think it was worth much, sleeping with him; I'd never been made to feel it was worth a whole hell of a lot, so why not? It didn't seem so very much to give after this pink house full of shiny beautiful kids. They were all so beautiful, his kids, and they had beautiful clothes: mauve and pink satin gowns like right off of television and I wanted to be like them so bad.

It turned out the house wasn't his; he was just caretaking. When the people came back we all had to leave, but by then it was too late, I was already hooked. I was somewhere where you didn't have to be watching out every single second who was behind you, who was going to try and steal your stuff, and who was going to try and put the make on you, and you'd have to talk your way out of it and they'd be crabby, not wanting to hear it, or they'd want to not do any asking or talking at all, but just take what they thought they deserved.

Winter knew all that. The irony is we gave him what we thought he was protecting us from, namely: we all slept with him, so we wouldn't have to sleep with other people we didn't like.

We gave him our space, so we wouldn't have to be alone. We didn't even think of it as protection really, it was just, like, we were a family and in families everyone takes care of each other and the father's supposed to take care of the children. It was just, like, not having to worry for awhile. And to live an ideal life. Because let's face it, we're all idealists. We all want utopia. A happy family. Not worrying, because there's nothing to worry about: because you're safe inside the family, and nothing bad can come in from outside. We were sick of being alone. That's what he really got us on. Sick of being lonely and alone.

It felt real too, except for the little bit of "what's wrong with this picture?" The part I still can't figure out is how he got all those people to do what he wanted. It was like some kind of sexual hypnosis. Why would a whole lot of people do what somebody else wanted? "The Father," they called him. "Because he's like that," they said, "like your father." Not like mine, that's for sure. He was like everything I'd ever wanted. Or at least, that's what I thought. Maybe he could do it because he had so much power that he'd taken away from other people. Maybe that's what the glow was.

Maybe we were all looking for an outside authority, instead of looking for it in ourselves. But what's wrong with wanting that? A nice father, someone who'll take care of you and know what's best. It's just a sham, though, just a lie. It doesn't exist now and I bet it never has.

Also, he was telling us we were magic, which in our deepest hearts we knew to be true. He was telling us our space was magic, and it is, maybe the only magic thing. I think, inside, that's what we'd wanted more than anything all our lives, was for someone to tell us how magic we were. We kept waiting and waiting to hear it, and nobody ever did. They just said we weren't smart enough or beautiful enough or too young or we were poor or we should fuck them, while all along there was a little voice inside going "Yeah, maybe that's true, but what about my magic? Can you do what I can do? Can you make things happen just by imagining them?" I bet not. And then Winter came along and said we could do anything we wanted, have anything we wanted, and he said what did we want, and so we said, of course, that we wanted to be stars. And Winter said he would make us stars. And we believed him, because, once you went into the fold, into the family, there was, like, this hum that permeated everything and it felt all soft and good like you'd just come and you believed it, believed anything was possible and maybe it was. All we had to do was fuck him. Of course, game over. 'Cause once you've given it away it's not yours any more, your power, I mean. You don't have to lose your power by screwing someone. I really believe that, that it should make you strong—but that's how he leeched you, was through the connection made by sex. Because once you're connected that way it can be really hard to break.

And once you've given away your power you can never be a star, no matter what. Not a real star, anyway. And I don't mean a star on television, although that's what he told some of the kids, the ones who wanted to believe that. I mean a person who shines with their own light, without giving it away to another.

I just headed away from it all one day and found myself going up the trail to Lydia's without having in mind that's where I wanted to go or even that I wanted to get away, just walking. When I got there things were different. For one thing, she was wearing clothes. A long dark blue thing, long skirt and big loose top. And her hair was out. Lydia had a lot of hair. There were a bunch of other women there too, her friends I guess, and they were all sitting around sewing. It was like a big quilt, and each of the women was working on a different section of it.

"What is it?" I asked.

"A star blanket," one of the women answered, and when I got even closer I noticed they were getting the cloth for it out of their clothes. When they needed a new section one of the women would take some scissors and cut a big section out of her skirt.

"Why are you cutting up your clothes?" I asked, and they all laughed.

"Oh, lots more where this stuff comes from," and I remembered having heard somewhere in my travels that the universe is constantly expanding. And when I got even closer I saw that they were embroidering the cloth in silver thread. I could make out all the constellations and a lot more I've never heard of. That blanket looked very warm, and more than anything I wanted to sleep in it, but I sat on the bench and sang with Lydia and her friends, watching them work. Then when it got so late I wouldn't be able to find the trail home by myself and they couldn't work anymore they lay it down on the ground and wrapped me up in it, and I lay beside the fire wrapped up in that star blanket, and listened to the women singing and laughing until I fell asleep.

It was the best sleep I've ever had. I dreamed the blanket floated up into space, spreading itself out across the sky, and I went with it, travelling to galaxies no one's ever been to, or even seen, only space wasn't cold like they always said, but the warmest place I've ever been, and that's the night that cured me of Winter and other predators like him for good. After that it was like I had another eye, a special eye that would tell me who was safe to hang with and who wasn't, and I've never really gotten in any more trouble since.

THE END

26

WHAT WOULD HAVE to happen for me to start calling myself a woman? I remember asking that.

Looking back, I think maybe it was the day of my healing. And not because I was older, but because I was more complete. It was later that day that I had started collecting stories, a project that has come to shape me. It feels like there's a connection, because of the missing parts of myself that I found that day, and as the stories came to me.

Back East again. Another year that seems like forever, but somebody told me all the years seem like forever when you're a teenager. I'm living in Toronto, at a well-run squatter co-op. After that healing camp was over, I caught a ride east, thinking I'd look for Lark. Skinny went up to B.C. to go to school with Estevan some more. Keep learning how to design and build renewable energy systems, with the emphasis on cheap, built out of junk as much as possible. Both portable and stationary.

I'm almost nineteen. Next month I get to drink legally. More fun than Girl Guides! I've been back East for over two years now and never heard from any of those people. There aren't so many Tribe message boards like there used to be; I can't even find their main website now. Things have broken down even worse.

But I try and make the city things more like country things, like it was there. Not having a home on the mountain was always sort of like having a home anyway. On the mountain you could make a fire, a lean-to, or some kind of shelter if you didn't have a tent. You could find something wild and green to eat to round out your bulk sacks of brown rice and black beans. You could eat at the community kitchen and chop carrots or wash dishes to contribute. There were lots of people there who knew what wild foods and plants you could eat and make tea out of and what they were good for, and were willing to take the time to tell you. Another workshop, one of the better ones I took. I remember almost everything I learned in it.

The people that gathered on that mountain were easier for me to get along with than city people, even if I didn't exactly like everything about them. But they had a code. Like the food; they always had communal food there. Even if a lot of people had their own food that was better, there'd still be some shared food, even if it was just homemade flour tortillas and macaroni without the cheese. And they'd have those bins full of clothes people lost or didn't like anymore, so people who came without enough to wear could find stuff.

I don't know why but people here don't seem to know about all that stuff. And so I tell them, show them. I remember how, on the mountain, by August when new kids showed up, I'd gotten to the point where I could recognize the fear, even if they kept it well hidden.

You'd have to show them, little by little, that they could make it. That most of it was really simple: keep your shitters far away and downstream from the spring; wash your hands before you do food prep; use condoms every single time. The raspberries are mostly over but the leaves make great tea. Mostly it was me and Skinny who talked to the new kids. They trusted us, because we were their age or just a little older. We had tattoos like they did, or at least Skinny did.

I stayed till Labour Day Weekend, when Skinny went north. In July and August, I wrote a lot of other people's stories there. I guess I had nothing else to do. I didn't know anything about satellite linkups, packet radio, cooking for hundreds or healing, and after that post fell on my leg when I was helping build a new outhouse that time, I wasn't much use for physical labour.

I couldn't even go on my beloved day hikes much anymore, so I wrote down people's stories. I guess I did it 'cause I always liked to write and it seemed so interesting to me, that everybody had a story, all those two thousand people there, especially the teenagers. Everybody's story was different and yet they were all so ephemeral, like the people would leave and go somewhere else, down the mountain to one city or another, or up to Canada, and their stories would be gone with them.

It amazed me how, beyond the surfaces, which most times was all you got to know, every one I talked to at the gathering had a life, as real to them as mine was to me. I didn't ask people to tell me their life story, although they could if they wanted. But mostly they just told me something that had happened to them, something that stood out, maybe only at the time we were talking.

I'm glad I did it, 'cause now I have something to show for that time; all their stories like jewels. I'm going to school now, doing Independent Studies through that college where you can do school even when you're on the road. I edited and collated all the interviews and stories and had them printed and bound into little books. They're going to be part of my thesis, but I don't think I'll ever stop thinking like a Tribe person now. If I start travelling again, I'll take books with me and have something to trade or give away or sell.

It wasn't like I thought it was really important or anything; I wasn't looking for something important to do. It was pleasure that led me there, the pleasure of their stories, their lives, and of how they all spoke differently, used words, those amazing things, in such different ways. I'd transfer them from my notebook or an iPod Skinny lent me onto his laptop in the orange Security tent. I'd go there after our morning talk, when he was out doing his rounds, checking up on everyone, keeping the peace. And at night we'd both sleep in that tent, never touching.

At the end of August we both quit drinking coffee mainly because there wasn't any, and after that, when he was finished his rounds, he'd make tea for us. It was usually something that grew there, like raspberry leaves or catnip or another wild mint or some kind of pine needles.

During the Perseid meteor shower we stayed up till morning, walking and talking. "If your mom was here, we'd do a packet meteor scatter," I remember him saying.

"A what?"

"We did it in Victoria this time last year. You bounce radio signals off meteorites and then see if you can pick them up again somewhere else."

"Cool," I said. "Can we do that?"

"Well," Skinny said, "you need different packet groups in different places working together. And there probably are some. But I don't know enough to try anything like that on my own."

We both stood there quietly after that, contemplating life without Laureen, each of us for different reasons. The heavens seemed to hear our thoughts, though, because for the next few minutes there were more shooting stars than I've ever seen in my life. If we couldn't have my mom, we had that at least.

After that I wasn't afraid of anything; I thought I could stay on that mountain forever, eating whatever and making clothes out of bark. Even without Skinny I wouldn't have been afraid. I wouldn't have been afraid of anyone or anything because I could see what they were, just another story, and how even in the worst person there is an understanding of it, even of the reason they had for the thing they most regret doing. It's funny, but almost everyone I talked to had at least one thing like that. And we were all living on the mountain together; that was what we shared. It was like some new kind of city, certainly run as efficiently, and even boringly, with its endless committee meetings and job charts that in the end somehow did manage to keep things moving.

There were no deaths, neither by accident or homicide or illness. Well, that's not true of course. But the homicide that happened, happened off-site. It wasn't Skinny's fault. He wasn't being derelict in his Security duties. There was only one knife fight, and Daniel broke it up before any damage was done. The theft was all minor, and there was very little of it.

Everyone left knowing more about how to look after themselves and each other than when they arrived. Yoga. Basics of herbalism. Build a still. Build a stage. Build a sauna. Make your own tinctures. Power your stage from bicycles. Convert your car engine to run on homemade bio-diesel. Speak Spanish. Write English.

I don't think anyone learned it all but even the laziest or most fucked up learned a little.

Once he got used to me, Skinny and I held hands a lot, and sometimes he would reach across the space between us and touch my face. On our log pile or at Circle we'd sometimes kiss, but at night in the orange tent he never touched me. Sometimes I thought maybe the idea of sex even with me reminded him too much of something he'd rather forget. He was a good kisser though, tasting of coffee and cigarettes; probably the only guy there that did.

I used to want him though, so bad. Boy, did I lust. I hadn't had sex yet, but all the same, or maybe because of that, I would think about it all the time, wondering what it was like. Of course there were other offers and I considered the free condoms box, the offerers, but in the end it seemed pointless if there was a guy there I wanted so much and couldn't have.

I changed my mind about that, finally, last year. A nice guy, already a friend, attractive but not like I'd imagined it with Skinny, not like it was when we did it in my dreams. That was one of the most beautiful things that ever happened to me, and it didn't even really happen.

I wonder if we ever did it in his dreams. If we did, he never told me, but then I never told him either so that doesn't tell you anything.

27

MY FATHER IS HERE. We're friends in a distant kind of way. I never could take him seriously after he didn't forward his new contact info that summer. He lives in my co-op. We both share little loft apartments with other people. He doesn't take care of me or anything, but sometimes at night he comes down to the common room and plays songs he was a little bit famous for, mostly in Europe, a long time ago. I always go and listen to him when he does that, and as time goes by I like my father's songs more and more. "Camden Town" has been known to make me cry in public more than once. So maybe it is through his music that he cares for people. Laureen said that once and now I understand what she meant.

Let it all go. Only then can you heal. In fact, letting go is a pretty good definition of healing.

Wish I had Skinny to tell that to. I remember all our conversations on the log pile, drinking his secret coffee, trying to puzzle it all out. Wanting to touch him but afraid of making him flinch.

Last week Lark told me that Laureen hadn't gone to San Francisco to reunite with Peter, but to confront him. She wasn't moping because she missed him, but because I'd finally gotten through to her. She was busy those first days not just setting up packet radio but simmering, alternately with rage and self-incrimination.

I don't know why it sunk in there and not all the times before.

Maybe it was the mountain. They say it's a holy place, brings necessary changes.

That's what she said the day we arrived. Maybe it turned out to be true, even for her. Sacredness, after all, includes truth.

Except then she had to screw it up, go look for him.

Bad idea, Mom.

She got herself killed.

The day they told me she wasn't coming back, they didn't have all the facts. When they found her body, it took them a while before they even figured out who she was. The case wasn't sorted out till long after I left the camp. And when they finally did figure out it was Peter and notified Lark, he didn't tell me. Until now, that is.

Spare the child.

But at least it explains why I had so much anxiety about her around that time. And it could explain what I experienced during my crystal healing.

So it looks like I should've gone up to Vic with Skinny like he asked me to, learned something useful. I guess I thought I still needed a little more parenting. Too bad I didn't get much, but one thing I've learned is that some people just don't know how, and all the things Lark gave me aren't the things you really need to grow on, even though he's nice in his way. Those necessary things I got from Laureen; they came alongside her moods, her poverty and dirtiness, and her broken down trucks. At the time I didn't know they were gold. I was busy being angry.

I remember the day Skinny told me who had raped him as a child. It was the same day he told me I must be some kind of healer because I was the only person who had ever been able to get it out of him. And yes, no surprises there, for Peter followed Laureen to Estevan's school at the end of that first summer we met him, when I escaped his groping hands to get back to Toronto to Lark. I wonder how I didn't see it sooner; probably because I was fretting about my mom.

Skinny's eyes that day were shadowed and his dolphin lips didn't smile. Still, after he told me we found something to laugh about and then he turned his tin cup over on our Second Meadow log pile and walked away into the Lodgepole pines like always.

And that's my story.

Acknowledgements

Thank you to the Ontario Arts Council who funded the writing of this book via its Writers' Works In Progress program. The original manuscript, *Drastic Travels,* eventually became this book as well as the novel *The Alphabet Stones*. Thank you to Doug Back, Anita Buehrle, Oliver Kelhammer, and Esther Pflug, who all provided me with insight into packet radio and other technical aspects of Laureen's work; any mistakes are my own. Thanks to Candas Jane Dorsey for structural comments. Thanks to Luciana Ricciutelli, Renée Knaap, and Val Fullard at Inanna Publications; I'm proud to be part of the Inanna family. Thank you as well to Anita Buehrle for her enthusiasm; we all need great readers and Anita is one of mine.

The stories Camden/Ameythyst gathered while on the mountain were previously published in slightly different form:
"Looking for Sofia" first appeared as "Lydia," in *Room of Own's Own*, Volume 19.1 (Spring 1996), Domestic Blissters.
"Secret Campground" first appeared in *The Peterborough Review*, Volume 1.2 (Fall 1994), Shelter Issue.
"Seeds" appeared in Windowspace '91, a storefront show in Peterborough, Ontario (Fall 1991) curated by Jo-Ellen Brydon, with an accompanying videotape by the author entitled "The Red Suitcase."

Photo: Anita Buehrle

Ursula Pflug is the critically acclaimed author of the novels *Green Music, The Alphabet Stones, Motion Sickness* (a flash novel illustrated by SK Dyment) and the story collections *After the Fires* and *Harvesting the Moon*. She edited the anthologies *They Have To Take You In* and *Playground of Lost Toys* (with Colleen Anderson). Her short stories and nonfiction about books and art have been appearing for decades in Canada, the U.S. and the UK, in genre and literary venues including *Lightspeed, Fantasy, Strange Horizons, Postscripts, Leviathan,* LCRW, *Now Magazine, Bamboo Ridge, The New York Review of Science Fiction,* and many more. Her work has been shortlisted or nominated for the Pushcart Prize, the Sunburst Award, the Aurora Award, the 3 Day Novel Contest, the *Descant* Novella Award, the KM Hunter Award, and others. Visit her on the web at http://ursulapflug.ca.